# CALUM TOD

# CALUM TOD

Norman
Malcolm
Macdonald

CANONGATE
1983

Canongate Publishing Ltd.
17 Jeffrey Street, Edinburgh

First published by Club Leabhar Ltd. 1976
Reprinted with emendation
by
Canongate Publishing Ltd. 1983

© Norman Malcolm Macdonald 1976, 1983


ISBN 0 86241 044 4 Cased
0 86241 043 6 Canongate Paperback

*The publishers acknowledge the
financial assistance of the Scottish
Arts Council in the publication of
this volume*

Typeset in 11/13pt Bembo by Witwell Ltd., Liverpool
Printed by Redwood Burn Ltd., Trowbridge
Bound by Butler & Tanner Ltd., London and Frome

*He who knows the male, yet cleaves to what is female*
*Becomes like a ravine, receiving all things under heaven,*
*And being such a ravine*
*He knows all the time a power that he never calls upon in vain.*

Lao-tsze
*Tao Tê Ching*

# 1

# ANNA

She smelled her fingers as she lay in the deep dark of the closed bed. The mattress of straw beneath Ann and her husband was full of lumps; Calum had slept on it since October and today was the Tenth of May; the first day of the herring fishing season. She sniffed at her hand; it was as though she were back again at the gutting board, the short knife twisting, the herrings flicking into the barrels. Matjes, matje fulls, the grainy female roes and the creamy male sperm. She put her hand into her thighs again, touching the torn tissue; this time she smelled the blood. It did not bother her, but she knew herself to be disappointed and uneasy.

"Am I now a woman?"

She whispered the words in the closed darkness and turned her head towards the humped shape of her husband beside her.

She had married Calum twelve hours ago and he would sail today with the turning tide from below the croft for the land of the Buckie men and he would not come back for six months. His Zulu fishing boat was long and round bellied and the mast thrust seventy feet into the sky.

Should she knot a woollen thread for him?

The brown-dyed nets were already piled in the hold of the *Boys Delight*. Ann would remain on the croft when Calum had gone; it was she who would look after the animals—and the reaping too when the time came for that.

She heard the movements of the strange cow down below in the byre end of the long cottage and knew it was time to get up. She drew aside the bed-curtain and stood on the calfskin rug. Behind the curtain on the other bed she could hear the quiet breathing of Kate, her sister-in-law and her best friend. Ann drew the marriage nightgown over her head and folded it carefully on top of her wooden kist. Her body felt strange to her this morning as she stretched her limbs; extended, as though she could feel all around her without touching, even as far as the plastered walls of rough stone.

*Tiocalach*, she thought. Ticklish sensations ebbed and flowed under her skin. Chickalook! That was how the young English fisherman had pronounced the strange Gaelic word. Laughing. At them and not with them, so Kate said. Ann never laughed back at the stranger when he made his rough approaches; she knew that the coming together of man and woman was too serious for laughter. But her eyes always turned to the familiar island boats when they nudged in to the quays of the mainland ports. Now she should know—but what did she know? In a few hours Calum would go and leave her alone and what did she know of man and woman together that she had not known yesterday? The minister spoke to them of sharing, but what can you share with someone who is gone away from you?

She pulled a short white petticoat over her head and then stepped into a voluminous grey and black striped skirt; she rolled on grey wool stockings and tied them above her knee with garters made from strips of cloth. Then the polka blouse and the black shoes and she was ready. The white *currag*, the mutch of her new married status could wait until Calum had gone. Instead, she covered her head with a crimson shawl, Kate's marriage gift. The crisp material rustled with a peculiar sound as she moved her head; she felt suspended between the old and the familiar and the new and the strange.

Ann went down into the main room, guided by the glow from the banked-up fire on the raised hob in the middle of the floor. She turned the dull red peats back to back with the iron tongs and crouching, blew on them. They flamed up and she put dry peats around them. She hung a black, three-legged cauldron from the soot-furred chain suspended from the chimney hole and then went outside to fetch water from the row of covered pails that stood on a wooden platform by the door. The cow lurched to her feet as Ann passed through the byre-end, alert to the creak of the wire handle against the heavy tin pail.

"You'll get something soon," Ann told her. The cat rubbed herself fiercely against her, the cow stared suspiciously at the strange woman, and a black collie stretched himself shyly from the straw.

She went back into the main room and found the meal kist after some searching. Calum would need porridge before setting out on his journey. A long and difficult sail in a fishing boat; she had done it, going to the herring, and now she remembered the constant motion; the elation and the fear and the sickness. Six months away from home, from her. Six months ago was last year—a lot had happened in the time. How much could happen in the next six months? People would be born and people would die and people would wed and some would not wait. But he would return. Six months. She would have the corn stacked and the potatoes lifted when he came back, it was that far in the future. Six months...

She got out a small tin basin from beneath the dresser and tipped some warm water into it from the cauldron. She washed her hands and face and then kilted up her skirt to perform what she knew would be the first rite of many; the washing, afterwards. She did not yet name what she and Calum had done together. What Calum had done to her? The warm water was very soothing. She applied some soft soap and then washed it off, quickly. It stung and she felt it to be dangerous to the life that may have started inside her.

She thought of the cows and the other animals together; how passive the females were. But she had seen, more than once, a cow in heat, angry and impatient, mount the ponderous bull. There were the jokes around the barrels, jokes that would have made the English-speaking curers blush, could they have understood them. Ann dried herself slowly, wonderingly.

She stirred the meal into the chuckling water and when the last handful had been absorbed she scraped the remaining grains from the palm of her left hand with the wooden spoon. Ann heard, for the first time, the chink of her wedding ring. She took a metal spoon from the dresser drawer and stroked the palm of her left hand with it. Chink, chink, chink, in the silence, louder now; a reminder that she belonged to Calum for ever. Such a long time...

He appeared in the bedroom door, silent on stockinged feet, fully dressed but for the leather seaboots. Looking at him now, his alien white body once more covered in comforting wool jersey and rough brown trousers, Ann no longer felt him as a stranger. The dark blue jersey was the same as those worn by all the other fishermen but Ann could always recognise his, through a forest of masts or moving along a crowded quay. It was right that he was going away to the fishing as he had always done.

"There is a good breeze from the west and you will catch the tide," she said.

"Very good, *a ghraidh.*" Calum smiled at her, sitting on the bench drawing on the heavy boots with easy pulls. He stamped his feet into them and went out. She heard him mount to the thatch at the end of the house where he could see the tide making in the Bay of the Boats.

When he returned she had a bowl of porridge and one of milk ready. He sat at the table and ate; she watched his loaded spoon dipping into the warm milk and then slipping between his wet lips until both bowls were empty. He sighed and sat still for a moment. Then he stood up, big and fair and out of place.

"Come," he said to her. He picked up the cloth bag of food she had got ready and gathered up his jacket and his oilskins.

"Bring the fire, woman," Calum said to her.

She took the heart out of the fire and put it in a zinc bucket and covered it carefully with warm ash and dry peat. She looked at him then and he laughed and spoke gently:

"You will be fine now, the two of you here together!" He was glad of Kate, and Ann was too. He was laughing and proud to have two women under his roof waiting for him, his sister and his wife. Suddenly Calum was strange to her again; she did not know whether she wanted him to go to the fishing or stay behind, at home with her and with Kate. Her husband.

She said nothing; she turned and went out, carrying the fire for the boat. She felt the heat of it through her skirt. They went through the croft to the shore and she it was who measured the strength of the sprouting green shoots of the oats. She stopped and stared at the blurred footprints in the ploughed land, made at the time of the sowing. They were her own. Next year, should would have a mare to pull the harrow and bury the seed.

"We'll need to get a mare," Calum had said. "It is not known but you may be heavy in the spring that is coming."

He was well ahead of her now, his step quickening and his nose raised to smell the sea and the shore tangle. He moved through the fields as though they did not exist. His business was with the sea; hers was with the land. She thought again of the passive cows and the active bull and then of the impatient ones who anyway had to await the bull's pleasure. Only one thing was sure. You had to have two people, a partnership, a crew of two; a crew that did not break up at the end of the fishing season, but went on and on. "Until the day of death," the minister said. A man and a woman and each wanting something from the other.

Ann went on, suddenly conscious of the need to get the fire going in the cooking stove on board. The men would need it on the long haul north and east about, through the Pentland.

The boat was almost upright on the flowing tide. Calum was below, out of sight. The other men would not arrive for some little time. Such a little time left. Ann stood at the water's edge and stared at the boat. A man and a woman. How strange it is and how little time there was left to discover...

Ann kilted up her skirt, took a firm grip of the fire bucket, waded out to the boat, and climbed carefully up the ladder. Calum was sitting down on top of the heap of nets in the open fish-hold. For a long time they looked at one another – without words.

Ann felt the heat of the fire against her; she put the bucket down carefully on the deck. The fire flared and smoked in the still morning air and the tar on the deck beneath the bucket began to bubble gently.

"Come down," Calum said, standing up and reaching his arms up to her. For an instant she stood fearfully on the edge of the coaming. Then she sprang straight at him...

She felt the pleasant roughness of the nets against her skin. The pungent smell of the bark in which they had been soaked went through her head. The tide picked up the boat and she felt it bump and then swing free beneath her. Behind her closed eyelids she was aware of a pink darkness.

Then she saw the fish moving, uncountable silent marchers moving through darkness. The bright shoal was endless, hanging above her and around her and beneath her in the luminous dark. The glittering bodies moved on and moved on and moved on and moved on; they streamed around her everywhere. The ocean was now a heavy weight, bearing down on her breast; but she breathed deeper and deeper and deeper and she began to rise at last, slowly at first, then faster and faster and faster until she burst through the white blazing surface of the sea with a great cry of release and triumph.

# 2

# ANGUS

His father came ashore one day from fishing and found the factor's men tearing the thatch from the cottage. He put the family in the boat and Angus was carried aboard in the arms of his mother. Then the boat beat down the coast of the island and the man returned to the house of his father. There was nowhere else to go.

When Angus was twelve he was coiling in the boat for the bay fishing. One day in the depth of winter, during a lull in the blizzard, they went out together to fish, the man and the boy. In the village, only meal and potatoes were left. Angus was barefoot and wore a thick wool gensey and a pair of his father's trousers with the legs cut off.

They laid a single line off Struipear and then the boy crouched in the bow. His legs and hands went slowly numb in the bitter cold.

After a long time, the man began to pull on the heavy line. It was alive with cod and ling. Angus stumbled aft and joined him in the stern. He worked beside his father, hauling and coiling, stunning the twisting fish, dodging the big hooks. Once, he slipped and fell into the slithering mass around his feet.

His sister Ann met them at the shore, skirts kilted up to avoid the deep snow. She carried a creel and as she tilted her body forward, it sat snugly on her hips.

She carried the fish home and cleaned them, setting aside the roes and livers for the first meal. Ann handed Angus a number of the smaller fish and he carried them on his fingers to the cottages of the neighbours.

Later, he drank the scalding fish soup from the cauldron and it burned his lips. But it warmed him and after a time he could feel his toes.


Angus came on deck carrying a bucket and soap. He stood with legs braced, swayed with the ship and listened to the hum of the wind in the shrouds. The sails were tight-bellied in a following wind and he squinted to see Kenneth who was on forrard lookout.

He cursed once again the tough English mate, who had now split their watches because they were Gaels. A man needs to be with the people he knows and Dutchmen and Cockneys had little for him.

He fetched some hot water from the cook in the galley and then put the shirts in the bucket to soak. Sydney was only a week ahead now and each sailor aboard was getting the channels.

Back in the crowded fo'c'sle he shoved his way through to their corner and clambered into his hammock. They always slung together and late at night the murmur of Gaelic disturbed the other men, who shouted at them, incomprehensibly. They would be glad to get to Sydney, wash the taste of the ship from their throats.

The thud of a wooden bucket striking the deck brought Angus out of his hammock and out on deck again. The shirts lay in the scuppers now and the big Dutchman was preparing to wash his feet in the bucket. The familiar rage seized Angus and he rushed at the man.

He struck the unprepared seaman behind the ear and man and bucket rolled. The Dutchman rose ponderously to his feet. They started to circle each other on the tilting deck. Men gathered to shield the fight from the bridge.

Angus rushed again. He struck two terrible blows that raised lumps on his opponent's face. The Dutchman hit back and Angus lost the sight of an eye. They fell against the bulkhead and grappled. Angus broke free and hit out again, using his big fists as clubs.

Like a tired bullock his opponent sank to the deck under the blows. He knew he had done wrong and he raised his bloody head in surrender.

Later, the two big men laughed together and showed each other their split knuckles and the bruises on their faces. Kenneth brought them cocoa from the galley and they toasted each other, wordlessly.


The men walked clumsily across the field to the shingle bank, hot in their oilskins and leather seaboots. Yet it was Christmas. Under his arm, each one held carefully the shallow basket with the four hundred hooks, baited with shellfish. It was very dark and they moved by instinct over the familiar ground.

On the shore, they gathered in groups around their boats and waited for the laggards. An old man who was there because he could not sleep listened to the sea moving on the invisible cliffs and muttered. A young fisherman laughed, loud in the quietness.

The first crew complete, the men put their shoulders to the boat and it grated over the stones and floated. After the first one, the rest left in quick succession, ten boats in all, leaving the old man alone on the beach. He listened to the splash and creak of oars, the fading voices. He called after them, but nobody heard him.

The first boat discovered a breath of wind beyond the headland and the brown sail rose jerkily into the darkness. The sky was dark beyond blackness and the man at the tiller was steering by ear and memory.

Angus sat by the dying fire in Ann's cottage. She was married now, with children, but she found room always for her wandering brother, whenever he chose to appear. The cottage then became a meeting place for the people who gathered to listen to the yarns of the returned sailor. Now and then, Calum would take the pipe from his mouth to ask Angus a question.

He had told them tonight of the shipwreck in the Pacific. Adrift for weeks in an open boat, burnt and starving, they had drawn lots to decide who should be sacrificed in the morning for the common good. Angus had lost and that night he lay in the boat with a knife in his hand. Before sunrise, in his delirium, he saw a sail, then woke to find it was real.

In the next village, the people had gathered to listen to the stories of Kenneth. They had come home together, after a lapse of years, the two shipmates, bringing tales of clippers and storms, strange people and places. But tonight, Kenneth was out with the boats, so that a friend could watch a sick cow. The neighbours went home early, except for an old man who waited uneasily on the shore.

The hurricane came out of the black North East and found the open boats across its path. Sails exploded, lumps of grey water came over gunwales, men shouted and plunged as they cut ropes and lines. The boats ran before the storm, blindly. Someone was bailing with his boots. A man began to pray and another took all his clothes off.

At first light, Angus went to the beach. Women were there before him, searching in the seaweed with numb faces. He saw through the surf on a tide bared rock, the skeleton of a boat. He plunged into the water and reached the sand bar.

He came across the first body within a few minutes. A boy, naked, his fair hair plastered to his skull. He lay, cushioned on the drying sand, fresh face upturned, grey eyes reflecting the sky.

Soon, Angus found another body, face down in a shallow pool. There was a familiarity about the way the man's arm rested along his side. Very gently, reluctantly, Angus raised the head and stared into the face of the drowned man.

Angus wept.


He was very tired, his lumpy shoulders bowed. The work on the shed by the shore had been hard on his old body. Angus sat on the doorstep and looked out at the bay. The sea was only ten feet away.

He ran his fingers over the ridges of scar tissue on his grizzled head and tried to think of a name for the new boat. The bay was a flat calm, as it had been at first on that night so many years ago.

There was still much to be done. A wife and a bed to move into the shed. The new boat, waiting for him on the other side of the Minch. As he stared at the still water, a word floated into his mind, then sank without trace. He wanted this boat to be well named. He knew now that she was the last one.

The mail steamer went out into the gale and then returned to the quay. They asked him to wait but he would not. Someone told him he was old, then backed away from the bunching of the gnarled fists. Angus and the boat disappeared into the murk.

On the other side the people gathered to comfort his widow.

Stolid fishermen shook their heads and shrugged. The sea looked bad in the grey morning light.

Ann was silent. He was her brother.

Late in the afternoon a scrap of sail showed between squalls. It came into sight again later on and it could only be him. At last, the little boat grounded on the beach. The old man was slumped in the stern and he did not move. They carried him ashore, tenderly, like a baby.

He named the boat *Tranquil*.

# 3

# MARTHA

I have always been told I was a doctor. Even as a little girl, here in Lewis, I knew I was different because I was the seventh daughter.

When my mother was carrying me, someone threw a ball of wool into her lap. The mark of the ball was on my cheek when I was born. I remember it very well—you could see every thread. I used to spend hours scrubbing my face with soap and water and staring into the mirror. But the brown mark never grew any less.

When I was seven my great-aunt died. My mother took me to the house where her body lay in bed waiting for the midwife. She put the dead hand on my face, on the mark. It was very cold but I was told that the mark would go away—as the body wasted away in the grave so that mark would disappear. I did not mind at all—I remember I was not the least frightened. All I was worried about was the ugly mark on my face that nobody else had. Every day after I looked into the mirror as soon as I woke up. I did not notice any change at first but gradually the mark began to fade. By the time I was ten years old it had disappeared. I do not know to this day whether the touch of the dead hand would make a birthmark disappear on anybody—or only on a seventh child—a doctor.

It must have been about this time that I cured my first patient. We are special doctors of course, and we only deal with one thing—something for which there was then no cure. Maybe there isn't a cure even now, in spite of penicillin and all the rest of modern science. The King's Sickness it's called, or King's Evil—a big lump full of matter on the patient's neck. It would go on and on and never come to a head and the sufferer would die sometimes if nothing was done. It was quite common in those days but I haven't heard of it for a long time now.

One day I came home from school and found a strange woman in the house. She was sitting by the peat fire with a cup of tea in her hand and I thought she must be a relation from across the island. Even when she came over to me and started to touch my face with her hands I thought nothing of it. But then I saw the angry lump poking through her hair—just behind her ear. She took my hand and made me touch the cyst and I was glad to do this for I remembered the terrible mark that had gone from my own face. Was it really true I could help this woman get rid of the Sickness?

The next morning my mother got me out of bed very early. She filled a large shallow dish that I had never seen before with water. It was just ordinary water from the well. She made me place my hand flat down in the dish, first forward and then sideways. I did this three times and my mother put the dish of water carefully away in a cupboard and locked the door. She did not spill a drop. Only then was I allowed to eat my porridge and milk.

We did this for three days and on the third day as I was eating my porridge I watched my mother pour the water carefully into a clean bottle. She told me that the water was now ready and that I would have to go with her to the sick woman's house.

I was glad—because I wanted to help the woman and I knew that I could and also because it meant that I would not have to go to school for three days.

We walked all the way to the next village about four miles away. There were no cars or buses in those days and we could not afford to take a gig. When we arrived the woman was in bed for she had been feeling worse. Her hair had been tied up on top of her head and I could see the cyst very well for she had to keep her head twisted to one side on the pillow. I bathed the lump three times with the water from the bottle and after a meal of salt herrings and boiled potatoes we walked home again.

We did this the following day and on the third day: this was the last day and we decided to stay, for the cyst would burst after the third treatment. So we did not start for home after we had eaten—we waited for the cure to happen.

About three o'clock in the afternoon I was playing outside. I had made a kitchen with a piece of wood and some broken crockery at the side of the house and I was pretending to wait for the children to come from school and I had made a scone out of peat dust and water.

My mother came to the door of the cottage and she was excited, although she pretended not to be. I suppose she was proud to have a doctor for a daughter. She called me inside and I remember to this day how I felt. I never felt quite the same again, even when I cured the man who had come from Glasgow and the doctors there—medical doctors, of course—had given him up. I was wondering was it really true that I could cure the Sickness—and me only ten years old! And I felt a bit scared too, I must admit, though I do not know what it was I was afraid of. Anyway, up to the bed at the far end of the house we went. I could hear the poor woman crying out and I nearly ran away. My mother caught my hand and took me over to the bedside. The cyst had burst and the patient's sister was cleaning and bandaging the wound.

After that time there were many more people that I cured of the King's Sickness. It was always the same—except that when I got older I prepared the water and visited the patients on my own. I did not need my mother's help after the first couple of times. Usually, the cyst would burst on the third day, though stubborn cases might require more than one course of treatment. I must have cured scores of people and, of course, I never accepted any payment. The silver sixpence was always returned to the patient after I had made a hole in it so that he could wear it about his neck. The trouble I had with those sixpences. . .

Once a man came from the Southern Isles—he was the only one I met who had tried the cure several times without effect. Now, as his was a special case, he had to get water from seven doctors before he could hope for a cure. I treated him just the same as anybody else but I did not expect a cure because I was only the sixth doctor he had been so see. I never heard how he got on. . .

It is ridiculous what they are telling me now. When my son went to register the birth of my grandchild the other day, the Registrar let him look up the family records kept in the town hall. There was a child they say—a girl who died after a few weeks, long before I was born. That means, they say, that I was not the seventh daughter and that I cannot be a doctor after all. It was my sister in America who was the doctor.

But I still say I am a doctor—I must be—I cured all those people didn't I?

# 4

# THE BOY

The boy's grandmother had been a strong woman, with broad hips and powerful legs. Her black eyes were rare in Lewis; later the boy was to hear the story of strange blood that had come into the islands from survivors of the Spanish Armada.

"The dark ones are very passionate."

Had a Spaniard been washed up on North Rona?

When the boy became aware of her, Ann's hair was grey and her powerful body was bowed. She had retired to her own room at the far end of the new white house that her son Donald had built in 1914. Now and then she emerged, in order to berate Fin who had married her seventh daughter, Martha, and to rescue the boy from his anger.

The boy liked to go to his grandmother's room. She brewed black tea in an enamel skillet sacred to the purpose. She gave him crisp crusts to eat, spread thick with the salty butter she made herself. Old Ann's few yellow teeth could no longer cope with crusts but she was superstitious about throwing them away.

The boy sat silently beside her and listened to her talk of the old times. He imagined what it would be like to sleep with her, under the heavy mound of blankets on the wooden bed in the corner, tucked between her big body and the wall.

But she never invited him to share her bed.

He saw her thighs once, heavy and sallow skinned. She was demonstrating to him the height reached by a sailor's seaboots. He never forgot this particular story of the drowned sailor who returned to the nets of her father's boat for three nights in succession, mutely demanding the return of the seaboots one of the crew had stolen from his corpse. On the third night, the guilty one threw the boots back into the sea:

"Son of the Devil, it is for the boots you have come."

The boy never forgot, either, the way his grandmother had swept the striped and billowing garment to the top of her thighs. Her wool stockings were fastened just below the knee with strips of cloth. For the rest, she was naked.

When Martha showed the boy the photograph he tried hard to remember his birthplace; tried to throw his mind back to the happenings that had started, for him, on the day after the picture was taken.

Glimpses came to him, short episodes. First there appeared the legless man. He was in a wheel chair, a tartan rug covering the empty space where his legs should have been.

The man on wheels spun around between the stacked shelves in the open-plan drugstore. He reached down the soft candy that his mother was buying for him. A few minutes earlier, the boy said:

"Put on hat and coat on, meet daddy, buy yum-yum."

Could he really remember actually using the words?

There was Alick, big and redfaced and cheerful on Saturday afternoons, when he came to stay with them for the weekend in the house on the raw street in Ontario.

One Sunday morning, the boy stood at the low window and gazed across the road at the big timber building which was such an odd shape. Alick came up behind him and bent down:

"All good Doolans go to church on Sunday."

He stood there for a long time, watching the people in their best clothes move in little groups into the mysterious darkness.

A sudden memory disturbed him. His mother lay in bed and he watched as a woman in white placed a dish between her spread thighs. Later, his father said:

"Another for the bootball team."

Was Fin displeased?

Words came to him, too. His father speaking to Alick:

"I started shovelling grain in the elevators with the Bohunks but I'm running the office now."

He travelled to Lewis from Canada in a big boat with his mother and the new baby. A woman behind a sheet of glass handed him a toy train. When they arrived, his aunt carried him ashore on her back. She wore a fur around her neck.

He could feel the softness of it on his palms.

He tore handfuls from it as they swayed down the gangplank, his legs locked by the arms of the sturdy girl beneath him.

The boy could speak only English at first and as his grandmother had never been to school she found it difficult to talk to him.

One day he broke the delicate arm of her spinning wheel in a fit of rage. Ann cried out violently to him in Gaelic; he recognised the word *briste* and screamed back at her:

"I'll *break* you!"

Martha came and patiently soothed them both, acting as peacemaker between the impulsive ones—her mother and her son.

She took the boy away from his grandmother's room and explained to him the value of the now irreplaceable object. Martha knew its value but could not name it for him, in English. The boy refused to listen; later, he was ashamed, but he did not tell old Ann he was sorry.

He had a year of wild freedom in the house on the island before his father returned from Canada.

He stood on the island pier and watched the boat dock and waited for a stranger to re-enter his life.

The boy was no longer the centre of the women's attention, now that Fin had come to stay. And he could not do as he liked; the heavy hand of authority was never too far away. In other ways he began to learn caution towards grown-ups.

His aunt was preparing to leave home and marry; she was going to town on the new motor bus and she asked him what she could bring him back.

"I want a car, please!"

"A car is it? And what kind of car?"

The boy replied at once:

"A car with a little driver in it!"

His aunt laughed and said she supposed such a car might be found in the Woolworth store that had just opened in town. The boy was worried; she may not have understood:

"A little driver... not made of tin. A little man made of meat!"

The grown-ups laughed at his simple request and relayed it to their friends. The car was a great disappointment to him also.

He now slept alone, accompanied only by the teddy bear who had travelled with him from Canada to the Hebrides. Night after night, he crouched down in his small bed in his parents' room holding Teddy and soon fell asleep. He could not conceive of going to bed without Teddy clutched in his arms.

But he was careless of the fate of his small friend during daylight when he often forgot Teddy's existence. This led him to his first confrontation with sorrow.

One day, Prince the collie found Teddy on the stairs and carried him outside in his mouth. He worried at the soft manikin for a time and this attracted the attention of the neighbour's dog. The boy watched as they fought playfully over Teddy, growling in their throats, their white-tipped tails flat on the grass.

Then the game became serious, the struggle got fiercer. Teddy tore apart across the chest, his sawdust innards blew into their eyes; they dropped the boneless velvet rag to the ground and walked away, snorting to clear their nostrils.

The boy rescued the remains; first there was disbelief and then came a pain that was almost too much to bear. He cried hopelessly for a miracle to restore Teddy to him.

The first day of school was an exciting one for the boy. He walked behind a bigger lad along the narrow gravel road until they eventually arrived at the schoolhouse. It was a long, whitewashed structure with many windows containing three large dusty classrooms.

All went happily for the first few weeks. His teacher was a tall dreamy girl with dark hair and the boy soon formed a warm feeling for her. She gave the six new scholars a book with words and coloured pictures. They all sat together at miniature tables, behind the desks of Infants One and Two.

The book was about two English children who spent their holidays in a strange place known as Richmond.

In the playground, the children spoke Gaelic but in the classroom only English was used. The boy had much less difficulty than his friends as he had learned English in Canada.

At some time during the third week, the boy had to go to the lavatory. He stared down at the small pedestal with interest; it was totally different to the concrete trench in the byre behind his home. In the first place it was far smaller and he dimly perceived that his aim would have to be perfect. It did not occur to him that he should sit on the cold porcelain; he had learned to squat and now he took down his shorts and squatted carefully, lining himself up in front on the small basin.

In spite of his efforts to look over his shoulder and direct the operation his aim was poor, the target was unsighted, the ammunition soft.

When he finally unbolted the door to walk guiltily away he knew he had messed up his hitherto unblemished school record. And he had been seen; later that day the headmaster marched him outside into the yard and humiliated him by pointing angrily at the brown stains.

Thus began the boy's education.

The boy formed the habit of going on short expeditions all by himself and his favourite spot was a long tongue of sandy land about a mile away that belonged to the local farmer.

The farmer lived in a huge crumbling and ancient house that was hundreds of years old.

Someone told the boy: "Lord Macaulay's great grandmother was born in the farm house," but, as he did not know who Lord Macaulay was, the boy was not interested; his interest in the old house was confined to trying to keep out of sight of it when on the farmer's land, for old Lane was known to be opposed to trespass.

The farm was very unusual in that it was almost entirely surrounded by the sea at very high tides, and at such times the boy could imagine himself safe on a tropic island.

His dream was to catch and tame a young rabbit, if possible one of the multi-coloured ones that were starting to appear due to the escape of a black and white buck who had decided his hutch in the town was too small for him.

The boy would lie quietly in a hollow and watch the young rabbits sporting on the turf. When he judged that the time was ripe he would rush into their midst and throw himself on his chosen prey.

He secretly hoped that one day a rabbit would stumble and fall before attaining its burrow so that he could catch it. But this never happened.

He was lying half-asleep in the sun late one afternoon when he was disturbed by the voices of some of the older boys from the village. They came over to him as soon as he sat up and they were smiling at him, one or two were laughing. The leader came right up to him and informed him joyfully:

"You are going to get it for stealing old Widow Alex's key."

The words did not register in his mind at first but as they were repeated with little variation he began to feel frightened. Where had he been all afternoon? Why here, among the sand dunes, watching for rabbits, all by himself.

His confusion grew under their watchful eyes and he could see they did not believe his weak denials. Perhaps he had gone to the Widow Alex's house at some time and had forgotten?

The older boys seemed so sure that he had done something; perhaps, without knowing it, he had made some kind of mistake? But he could not remember having been at Widow Alex's house. In his mind, she now became confused with his grandmother; a sturdy woman with a strange smell, wearing a billowing skirt of grey and black stripes.

The boy turned for home, reluctantly dragged himself up through the narrow croft, past the startling deep green of the potato field, past the secretly moving and whispering oats, past the sour land next to the house which his grandfather's best efforts had failed to drain.

He could see the house now, standing next to the gravel road, one of a row of similar two-storey buildings. Light blue smoke was pouring from the chimney at the road end; his mother had made up the fire with fresh peats and soon she would start to prepare the family's tea. Mealy pudding, broth and mutton, fresh plaice, salted fish? It did not matter to him now, he was not hungry, his inside felt tight and strange.

Yet he still did not fully believe in his situation; did not fully accept that he was to be accused by authority of such a despicable action, in spite of the assurance of the elder boys. In the village, a neighbour's property was sacrosanct; to be found guilty of theft from a neighbour was to become a despised outcast.

Young as the boy was, these near-mystical ideas of community living had been impressed strongly upon him by his father, who held to a fanatical belief in personal integrity, based upon pride, the bitterness resulting from the shattering of his dream of a post-war world of opportunity and by the memory of the obscene holocaust he had so arbitrarily survived.

The boy was now aware of this only very dimly but he knew that his father was powerful and that he would ensure that right was done. But what if he, the boy, had in some unexplainable way somehow offended Widow Alex, had indeed done something wrong to her cottage, to her door, to her lock and to her key?

He had been told with deep conviction that he had been seen that afternoon near the Widow Alex's cottage. Had he really been there and had he now forgotten? Guilt lay with a heavy weight in his small chest as he stepped reluctantly into the cool dusk of his home.

The boy's father was more puzzled than angry. He had already heard the accusing story of Lonnie, the boy's friend.

"He saw you take it!"

The boy shook his head. He glanced up at his father's face and dimly perceived the struggle in him. This was not a simple family matter that could be dismissed with a couple of painful clouts around the head, a release that the boy prayed for now, knowing also that it would not come. Other people were involved, penetrating the privacy of the family.

There was the boy Lonnie, son of an incomer and stranger to the village; the Widow Alex, who had been shocked by her loss into toiling painfully through the village in order to report it to the headmaster; the headmaster who ruled his pupils with Old Testament severity, under the approving eyes of the parents.

And the headmaster was someone that Fin respected; the boy had seen them deep in conversation together. These men were the most powerful figures that existed in the small boy's world.

"Come with me!" said Fin and the boy followed slowly, his head down.

Fin knocked on the door of the cottage diagonally opposite the Widow Alex's and questioned the trembling maiden lady who came to the door. She was pathetically pleased to be of help but she had seen nothing and this was not surprising. The view of Widow Alex's cottage from her house was blocked by a barn.

"But this is where Lonnie said he was standing when he saw the boy take..."

Fin's bottom teeth moved forward to grip his upper jaw, a habit of his when thinking reflectively. This quirk was facilitated by the absence of his two front teeth—knocked out years before by a sledge-hammer when he bent too close to a spike whilst working on the abortive island railway.

The boy said nothing but his spirits rose and he began to believe once again in his own innocence. His father's all-knowing wisdom would ensure that justice was done to him. He waited for a pronouncement from his father, a decision to report his findings to the headmaster that would put the matter beyond further doubt.

But none came. On Monday the boy had to go to school and face the promised inquiry. Nothing further was said to him by his father who seemed content to leave the matter to the good sense of the headmaster.

The young ones filed into the classroom after the bell and were set to reading about the family who spent their holidays in Richmond. The boy saw the teacher's eyes flick over him when she chose the favoured ones who read to her. He was glad in a way; he knew his voice would have betrayed him if asked to read aloud.

At last, the door opened and the summons came. Five boys were led through to the top classroom by the headmaster. They stood around his desk in a semi-circle, aware of the stares of the older pupils sitting at their desks behind them; it was as though everybody knew the guilty one already.

Lonnie was not among those to be questioned and there was no sign of him. The faces of the other four looked complacent and self-righteous to the boy. Obviously, they were not guilty of violating anybody's cottage. This left only himself and again he wondered if somehow—in a dream?—he had done something wrong, something involving a very old woman in a striped billowing skirt, short woollen stockings and heavy shoes. The other four were questioned in turn:

"Where were you on Saturday afternoon?"

The answers came, pat.

"Was anyone else with you?"

"Yes, sir."

One by one, the other four were sent back to Miss, leaving the boy standing alone in front of the headmaster. He could hear the faint creaks in the desks behind him as the watchful scholars stirred in anticipation.

The boy looked up at the face of the head, at the hawk nose and grizzled hair. The face stared back at him, speculatively. Abruptly then, the man turned, reached for the brass handbell on his desk and shook it violently. Immediately a great shuffling arose all around the boy as the school went outside for the morning break. After a few seconds, the head motioned to the boy to follow them and the bell gave a last, forbidding clang.

Outside in the playground, the boy watched the carefree play of all the others. They were playing harder than usual, shouting even louder. Nobody spoke to him or came near him.

He stood by one wall and stared dimly down at the shiny boots on the feet that connected him to the hard earth. The boots shone in the weak sunlight and he had a glimpse of his mother's vigorous polishing, silent in the early morning. His main feeling was one of desolation, of apartness, of wanting to be somewhere else.

But he knew too that there was nowhere for him to go. What he desperately desired was for things to return to the blissful state they had been in on Friday, and all through his life, so far as he could remember back. He would give anything, do anything, to get back to that.

The oldest lad in the school, a boy of fourteen, sidled up to him, tall and saturnine.

"Tell him you did it."

The boy did not answer but smiled uncertainly up to the fearless one who had dared to speak to the outcast in full view of the big school windows.

"Tell him you did it and he will let you go."

To relieve his agony of uncertainty. To admit to the crime and then be permitted to escape from the head's room, remove himself from the reach of the speculative eyes, the whispers. He stared at the dark face in front of him through moist eyes.

"It will all be over, then," said the voice and the face went away. The boy felt his chest heave in a great sigh and his vision cleared. He felt a little better in some strange way. "It will all be over." If only he could believe that?

He stood again in front of the headmaster.

"Where were you on Saturday afternoon?"

"Chasing rabbits on the farm."

"Was anyone else with you?"

"No, sir."

"Did you take the Widow Alex's key?"

The boy did not reply. His head fell lower, he bit his lips, his face felt fiery with shame. Could a grown-up of such power be wrong? He must be guilty, or else why was he standing here?

"Speak up, boy!"

A voice spoke and said "Yes." It was his own. "Can I go now, sir." He had not said that.

"What did you do with it?"

The boy's imagination came to his rescue. He saw himself throwing a huge iron key into the air. It fell with a silent plop into dark water among weeds.

"I threw it into the big pond."

"That was very wicked of you. A poor old widow must be protected from the likes of you, boy."

He said nothing more. Would he be left alone now that he had confessed? "It will be all over." Was it?

"Your father shall hear about it. You may go back to your room."

He stumbled through the door and went back to his desk. And he discovered quickly that it was not over at all.

His father came home from the town, riding a new bicycle. He jumped off at the roadside and called the boy to him. Fin took a small packed from his pocket:

"Here! Take this to the Widow Alex to replace the one you did away with." His breath smelled strangely.

The boy's mother came out of the house and frowned when she saw the bicycle. The boy saw that she also looked carefully at her husband's face but she said nothing. His parents walked away across the grass together, leaving him alone, standing by the roadside with the hard little parcel in his hand.

He took to wandering for long distances along the cliffs and sand dunes, seeking places where he would not be seen by those who knew.

The shores of the semi-circular bay were dotted with other villages; in them he was a stranger to the people.

He came to know many of these places in the company of the driver of a coal-merchant's lorry who started to take the boy with him on his rounds. Hefty was large and jovial, his brawny arms ingrained with a shiny patina of coal dust. He asked no questions of the boy who sat quietly beside him in the cab as he drove his laden lorry along the narrow roads, expertly avoiding the patient sheep and the flurries of panicky hens.

He gave the boy a lesson in the art of folding empty sacks and then left him to enjoy the thrill of the changing scene from the dusty cab of the green lorry.

One day they delivered ten sacks of coal to a cottage miles away from the boy's home in a village where he had never been. A smiling woman came out to meet them and led them round to the barn at the rear of the house.

The boy watched her as she stood by the growing pile of coal. When the man was not there, she looked pensive but she laughed with Hefty and replied to his sallies each time he reappeared with a heavy sack balanced on his bulging shoulder.

Hefty began to touch her, roughly, each time he emptied another sack. When he came with the last one he was breathing heavily and he threw it down at once, without bothering to pour it out. He reached for the woman and she took a slow step towards him. He gathered her in his arms with the same encompassing movement he used to place a sack on the edge of the lorry platform. He laid her down on the heap of coal, muttering quietly.

His right arm came down, his hand brushed up the woman's skirt. The boy saw the streaks of grey leap up on the white thigh. The woman's face was slack as she looked over the man's shoulder. Her eyes jumped out at the boy then and she cried out:

"The boy!"

Hefty turned angrily and the boy fled in panic, back to the lorry, where he stood, uncertain whether he should board it or not.

An older woman appeared at the door of the cottage and stood anxiously watching the barn. She was agitated too, and kept smoothing down her white apron.

The boy and the woman ignored each other, both were silent and distracted.

The others appeared at last, walking silently apart. Hefty motioned for the boy to get onto the back of the lorry and jumped into the cab. The lorry drove off at once; no delivery slip was presented, no money collected. From his perch on the coal sacks the boy watched the two women go into the house, after one wary look at each other.

Hefty never called for him again and ignored him on the one occasion he approached the green lorry.

The boy began to wet the bed. And one day, his younger brother called him Pissabed in the hearing of some lads.

The boy slowly came to realise that his feelings of alienation were not entirely due to his having confessed to the theft of the old woman's key. The incident had largely been forgotten, except by the boy himself, who was reminded of it every day he passed the widow's cottage on the way to school.

There were other factors at work and he began to become aware of them in arguments with his friends. The truth was that his father was strongly disliked by many of the village people, due to his outspoken attacks on anything that smacked to him of hypocrisy.

The regular churchgoers, who crept along the road every Wednesday at noon in their dark clothes, were one target. Seeing them, Fin would go out to his gate and call:

"Have you nothing better to do!"

Much later, the boy began to understand, but not yet, not now.

Fin was full of bitterness about what had happened to his Canadian dream. The world depression, engineered by ruthless financiers, had deprived him of his chance of becoming his own man. As the hopeless years ground slowly away, Fin turned his hatred and aggression outwards, against all manifestations of indifference to the problems of the blind poor.

And whenever the boy displeased him. Fin beat him.

Meanwhile he struggled to provide for his growing family. There was no work except fishing and Fin crewed for a time on the inshore boat that belonged to Angus, who was his wife's uncle.

But Angus was an even stronger personality and he owned the boat. He had sailed in his young days on the China clippers, had fought with his fists men of a dozen nationalities, had been adrift for weeks in an open boat in the Pacific, during which time he was reputed to have eaten human flesh.

Inevitably, he and Fin fell out and Angus was left alone to work his boat, a state of affairs that the stubborn old sailor welcomed.

Fin turned his attention to business and decided to open a shop. He built a large wooden shed between the house and the road; old Angus, still immensely strong, came to help and rolled the boulders into the foundation that Fin had dug.

The boy watched and wondered. But when the shop opened it was nice to go behind the counter, seize a hot loaf from the shelf, and take it in to his mother. The neighbours came to buy their groceries, often on credit.

Fin kept a notebook to record the small debts, a page to every family, each item set out in his flowing handwriting.

The boy was disappointed that his father no longer fished; now he could not stand on the shore in the early morning during the summer holidays waiting for the boats, certain of his entitlement to be there among the women and boys.

But old uncle Angus had his home there; he had built a shed for himself and his complaining wife only yards from high water and his last boat the *Tranquil*.

He still went, sometimes, and he was the first to bring news to the Outend of the finding of the body of a man who had walked to the rocks that same morning and stepped quietly into the calm sea.

As he hurried home with his story, he could see the wallowing shape under the still water, entwined in the pulpy fingers of seaweed. The crabs he was carrying rattled together. He threw them into the oatfield, horrified by his thought: crabs eat drowned corpses.

# 5

# SHONA

She was tall with dark hair and white skin and she smiled often although her husband was away at sea for most of the time.

They had married in Glasgow and when the week was done Murdo ran up the gangway of his ship. Shona returned to the island alone. She lived in the cottage where she had been born and later four little ones ran about her feet. Her mother was old but she looked after the children and Shona had time to feed the cattle and work the land.

One Spring, Murdo came home as always for a week, in order to cut the peats for the winter following. But the weather was hard with frost in the ground and peat must be cut when it is warm.

"I'll come back in May when the oil rises," he told Shona as they lay quietly in the bed that was not really big enough for both of them.

But he sailed on a long tripper again that year and no peats were cut. Shona wrote him a letter in the summer and he received it in, Rio. He put on his good suit and a white shirt for a run ashore.

"I've only got to hang my breeks over the end of the bed," he said to one of his shipmates.

Winter came in place of autumn to the island that year. The easterly gale went on for weeks, uprooting the weed from the sea bottom and piling it up in sheltered bays. The oatfields were flattened and twisted when still only touched with yellow.

Shona bound the slimy straw with numbed hands. She felt a movement inside her and straightened her back. The smell of the tangle made her think of spring and planting time. But you need a man to haul the seaweed ashore and help to spread it on waiting fields.

She bent down again and gathered another armful of the wet stalks. The seed was nearly gone, gorged by the seabirds who flew away to be sick on the rocks and returned to feed again, screaming and laughing about her.

There will have to be bought this year, dear bread from the baker in the town. There will be few oatcakes baked on the hot griddle over the fire.

Her heart kicked in her chest, harder than the child.

"Ah, Lord! I have no peats for the winter. And nothing to buy coal with either!"

Murdo was ashore in Tahiti half an hour after coming off watch. The French police were edgy, for an American ship was also tied up at the long wharf and the first fights had already broken out.

The noise in the bar was very loud and seamen and girls were milling around. A dark girl in a cotton dress with a flower behind one ear edged up to him. She said something in French and he bought some wine for her. She put a wreath of sickly smelling flowers about his neck and laughed up at him with red stained teeth. He ordered more brandy and washed it down with the watery beer.

The guitars boomed out again in the confined space. Two girls in grass skirts came out on to a small platform that jutted out from one wall, out of reach of groping hands. They swayed supple hips, bellies undulating to the pounding rhythm of the strange music. Their arms moved slowly around their quivering bodies and the skin under them was very pale. He wondered what their breasts felt like, under the flimsy cloths that bound them.

Murdo felt the hands of his companion on him, touching the pockets of his shorts. She found the wallet and rewarded him with another smile.

"Come?" she said. "You come?"

With a last glance at the sweating hula dancers, he picked up a bottle and let her lead him away through the press of brown women and excited, angry men.

The coalman left the engine of the lorry turning over while he shouldered the stiff sacks and poured them expertly on to the scar on the grass left by last year's peat stack. Each time he returned to the murmuring vehicle he flexed his lumpy shoulders and the muscles of his arms slid around under the shiny patina of coal dust.

He glanced out of the edge of his eye at Shona standing silent; her round belly stretched her apron. He paused to tighten the heavy leather belt about his waist. The steel buckle winked at her in the cold sunlight as he pulled his trousers, armoured in black dust, up around his crotch.

When he had built a glittering pyramid on the ground he shook out the empty sacks and laid them carefully on the platform of the lorry, neat as any housemaid. Shona turned and entered the barn; she stood waiting for him beside the heap of hay.

A worm of guilt gnawed at her. But we must have fuel for the winter! She wondered whether to lie down at once and was surprised to feel a flicker of heat in her body.

The coalman turned up the engine of the lorry to a near roar. The truck stood alone, shaking and throbbing in jealous anger. He went into the barn and closed the door carefully behind him.

Three weeks after leaving Tahiti they docked in Fremantle. As soon as they had tied up, Murdo went to see the First Officer.

He had noticed the ulcer the day before but he told no-one. Some of the men were proud of catching the pox, believing the scars to be badges of manhood.

Murdo knew about the canker that would silently work on his body and later on affect his mind and he was afraid.

The mate gave him a note and he went ashore at once. The doctor examined him with breezy Autralian tolerance.

"I'll give you 606, a double dose," he said at last, filling a syringe with yellow salvarsan. "Teach you to be careful where you dip you wick in future."

The child was born dead on St Bride's day and the elder put on his black suit and came to the cottage to read from the Bible.

Some of the men came later and carried the little box to the cemetery. They buried it with bared heads and no ceremony.

The knee-woman told Shona that the child would have been sickly and that her family was complete now.

"The womb has a hole in it," she said, pleased with her knowledge.

Shona wondered why the knee-woman should hate children.

"He had a mark on him," the knee-woman said and went away.

Slowly, Shona went outside and stood looking down at the small heap of coal that was left. She thought about the mark on the dead child.

She picked up a nugget of coal and held it in her hand. It was cracked and grey and it crumbled away in her fingers.

She brushed her hands together but the shiny dust clung to her palms.

# 6

# FIN

Life passed, memories faded. The headmaster died and another took his place, another war survivor.

He set the boy to pass his bursary and he was awarded ten pounds per annum for bus fares to the secondary school in town.

A week of strangeness was followed by two weeks holiday while sticky paper was pasted over the school windows. The Americans promised some ships and the first sad telegram came to the village. Fin delivered it personally; he was now the postmaster and the guardian of the telephone for the Local Defence Volunteers. One day he read for the boy the swift flicker from a ship ten miles away:

-W-E-L-C-O-M-E-H-O-M-E-J-A-R-D-I-N-

The grey shape was blotted out by the headland. Fin stared after it, his eyes fathomless, staring out over No Man's Land once more.

"God, I wish I was a heifer," he cried.

Uncle Donald was long dead, under a shining marble stone near the gate of the cemetery in the sand, lying by his father who had read the Bible by the light of the setting sun. Now old Ann waited for her call to fill up the lair. She told the boy why Donald had died, her only son in a parcel of girls:

"They had to row the captain back to his ship. It was an awful day, with a great storm. Donald, my Donald, was on an oar in the bow. They rowed and they rowed against the tide. Some of the men gave in, they put up over the side. The captain sat in the stern and he began to shout. But Donald now, he did not give up, he rowed and he rowed, into the waves. The ship came nearer and the sea got stronger. The captain shouted for the last time and Donald did his best. Something went in his chest, something tore inside him. But he did not stop rowing. When they got aboard, the skipper called out to the watch officer: 'Give MacLeod a double rum!' Then, after the war, the wasting disease came on him and him the finest boy in the village.''

His grandmother wept silently and showed him the ring Donald had given her; a thick gold band in the shape of a belt which she wore on the third finger of her left hand.

A daughter had been born to Fin and Martha at last. . .

The secondary was more anonymous than the village school and he hid successfully for most of the time among the forty pupils on One B.

The English master carried a leather strap over one shoulder, hidden under his jacket, but the boy never felt its sting.

He explored the town alone, the lively quays and the damp dead alleys. He saw a bloated corpse being dragged from the harbour and this glimpse of untidy death stayed with him.

He had his first orgasm, excited and fascinated by the discovery of his physical self; watching a girl from the security of the byre.

The boy had to go to Sunday school in common with nearly every other child in the village. The classes were taken by the elders in the mission house during the quiet period between dinner and tea.

The homework for Sunday school consisted of memorising in Gaelic two verses from a psalm and one answer from the Shorter Catechism, the latter invariably incomprehensible. The children went in awe of the elders, so most were able to gabble their answers when their turn came. This took up most of the hour allocated to the Sunday classes.

Once a year, as a reward for regular attendance, a *suaridh* was held, when bags of buns were handed round.

One Sunday, the boy rebelled and he hid in the byre next door. He was wearing his best suit, as always, and he moved carefully, so as not to stain it or his shiny boots. Through a crack, he watched his father walk home slowly from the shore, through the green croft, pensive in unaccustomed idleness. It did not occur to the boy to wonder why he had to go to Sunday school although his father never went to church. All he thought about was that he would be punished if found out. He wasn't, but the suspense was too hard to take and he never dodged Sunday school in this way again.

The doctor came again to examine his young sister who was suffering with pains in her side. His mother handed the boy a small bottle holding a warm yellow liquid:

"Take this to the hospital to be tested."

Martha was worried and Fin was distraught. They had desperately desired a girl child and now, at the age of four, she was suffering from something that the doctor could not discover. Her name was Maretta and she was fair and small and pensive.

The family grew closer together at this time. One night, the boy fought an older friend, head down, raining blows on the surprised youth's midriff.

"You asked for it!" His voice was choked.

He did not know why he attacked his friend. His fragile equilibrium had been disrupted since the mysterious illness struck the tiny girl, his unknown sister. Feelings had been forced to the surface and the boy was frightened; he did not know how to cope with the new and unusual access of emotion now displayed by his anguished parents.

The child was taken into the hospital at last. Too late? The surgeon's knife was to probe and cut the tiny female abdomen in order to release the poison that was gathered there.

Over the months, the family doctor had vacillated. At last, Fin's anxiety overcame his reluctance to question a man of superior education:

"I want a second opinion."

The doctor saved his face; he did not send a colleague but instead persuaded the surgeon from the hospital to accompany him to the village. Maretta was taken away in an ambulance within the hour and her parents began the vigil at the hospital.

The boy got tea for himself and his brother for the first time in his life and this alone was enough to impress him with the sad seriousness of the situation.

Maretta came back from the operating theatre and hovered between present and future. One night she began to whisper and

Martha bent desperately over the hospital cot to grasp the words: "A drink of milk." Much later, Martha wept as she remembered. But not yet.

The boy was lying in bed very early when his mother entered the room. She sat on his bed and said:

"Rise my dear and get ready. Maretta died at four o'clock this morning."

Something about his mother as she sat on the edge of his bed; it may have been the unfamiliar black blouse and skirt; it may have been the tenderness in her voice, her resignation, her courage and her weakness, her femaleness; something about his mother at that moment caused the boy to break into loud sobs. Martha pressed his shoulder:

"Hush. You'll waken your brother."

From downstairs there arose a terrible sound. Martha raised her head and listened. Then she said, quietly:

"Your best suit. And a black tie."

She found him a fresh shirt and brought him a black tie from his parents' room; the tie that Fin wore to attend funerals. He pulled on his stockings and shorts in a fever of anxiety. Already, he was feeling towards the knowledge that things were changing, for him and for the family.

When the boy went downstairs he found a neighbour woman stirring the porridge pot that hung in the fireplace. Everything felt strange and new and frightening. There was no sign of his father. Perhaps he was in the byre attending to the cattle? He could hear his mother's slow tread overhead. There was nothing to do but wait.

He went outside into the crisp September air and stood looking at the row of croft houses that stretched away from him on either side, hugging the gravel road. The men who had built them—men of his grandfather's generation—had been reluctant to use any more land than was strictly necessary for building on. They were desperate to use every possible square yard in the struggle to grow enough to keep their big families alive.

The narrow crofts ran side by side for half a mile till they met the sea. Beside each house stood the cottage of undressed stone that had formed the original homestead. Many of them were in bad repair, with sagging beams and rotting thatch, but they still served as barns and henhouses.

There were no trees anywhere, apart from one clump of sycamores planted at the turn of the century by a man who had spent his young days on Hudson's Bay. He had returned with a chest full of money, so they said, after his young wife had journeyed to the frozen north to fetch him, when it seemed he was in no hurry to come home. The barn he had built was the largest on the island.

The boy looked beyond the crofts to the sea and the huge bay; he noted without thinking that the tide was out; the long sand bar was exposed and it had that peculiar orange-coloured dryness which meant the tide was now due to turn back on the fill. A good day for rock fishing. But there would be none of that until after the... funeral. Suddenly he thought about school; would he have to take the crowded little bus today to the town as always? He went inside to ask his mother.

He did not go to school that day or the next. Soon, the house was full of women, neighbours and relations. They all brought something to eat or drink, adding it silently to the pile on the kitchen table. There was constant tea-making, the passing of plates, low conversation. His mother sat by the fire; her face sagged with weary sadness. She responded to the hand clasps and the muttered words with gratitude. Fin had not come back.

The boy went out, went around the back of the house, slowly, reluctantly, he approached the dead, closed and manure-crusted door of the byre. As he did so, he remembered the rabbits. And the bicycle.

The bicycle was old and shaky, a woman's. It had belonged to the boy's aunt, Fin's half-sister, who had passed it on to her young brother. This uncle, who was only seven years older than the boy, had eventually left it with him, after one of his visits. Ian came to the village occasionally, to see a girl he was fond of. The boy was delighted.

He pedalled along the main road, away from the town, towards the village that stood high above the White Sands. When he had panted his way to the top—he was too proud to get off and push—the boy could see the road falling away towards the beach beyond; it swooped down, bending gently, towards the narrow bridge at the bottom. It looked breathtakingly steep and he wondered if he dare cycle all the way down to the bridge.

To the right of the road, about half way down, a path led to the springy turf of the *machair*. Perhaps he could steer off the road into the safety of the sand dunes if he began to lose control? Carefully, he began the long descent.

As the speed of the cycle increased he began to have doubts. There was still another quarter of a mile to go. He applied the brakes and the cycle slowed. At that moment he heard a shout from a field by the roadside. An older lad of his acquaintance was working there, lifting potatoes. The shout came again and he saw the lad pick up several divots of earth and run towards him.

He began to pelt the boy with earth.

There was an easy escape from persecution this time. Exultantly, the boy put his head down and began to thrust hard with his strong legs. The bicycle surged forward and gathered speed quickly. Within seconds, he was riding fast, spinning down the steep road. The cycle began to shudder a little. He was still less than half way down. The turn off to the *machair* was speeding towards him. In a few seconds it would be too late to swing aside. He squeezed the brake lever. Nothing happened. The shuddering increased as though the cycle might fly apart. His eyes blurred with the whipping wind of his passage. He felt a great fear. The bridge disappeared from his misty vision now behind the bend.

The *machair* turn-off whipped past and as it did so he twisted the handlebars towards it. They were jerked from his grasp. He crashed into the gravel by the roadside in a sliding tangle of metal, fear and pain.

When he heard what had happened, Fin was very angry:

"You might have been killed!"

The boy's injuries were not serious; grazed knees and bruises. He did not tell his father about the lad who had thrown lumps of earth at him. But he knew that the action had been meant to get him into trouble on the hill.

"I'm going to lash that bicycle to the rafters in the barn," his father told the boy. But Fin did not do so. Nevertheless, the boy's pleasure in the bicycle was now spoiled.

A few days later, the lad who had so thoughtlessly endangered the boy's life came to see him. He was carrying a small birdcage. Three balls of fur lay entwined in the bottom of it, half-buried in straw. They were coloured black and mouse, strange piebalds; the unnatural shades of their fur proclaimed them to be wild rabbits born of a domestic doe. They were very young to be alone in a wire-barred cage.

The boy was fascinated and after he had handled them, the lad made his offer:

"I'll swop them for your bike."

The boy was tempted. He knew that his father would be angry—and not without reason. It was not a fair exchange. Three wild baby rabbits for a bicycle was a ridiculous bargain. Perhaps. The boy knew—and he half believed the truth of it himself—that this was the way the transaction would be seen by everybody. Most important of all—the cycle was a present; second or third hand it may be, but a present to him from his uncle nevertheless. He hesitated.

The lad was persuasive; seeing the hesitation, he began to play upon the boy's indecision. The boy had an anxious desire to please, to remove the tension of the moment; the lad intuitively recognised it. The lad was aware of Fin's reputation and his anxiety to clinch the deal quickly and get away safely added to his eloquence. He glanced about him:

"Hurry up, before your father comes."

He was making the boy his ally against Fin. Resentfully, the boy recalled Fin's threats to take the cycle away from him, to lash it to the rafters. His father had been wrong in the past; he had failed to protect him against the power of the headmaster. He had beaten him many times and only sometimes had he deserved it. The words were out:

"All right."

He helped the lad to mount the bicycle that he now fearfully realised he had practically given away. Standing on the pedals, the lad wobbled into the distance. What *would* Fin say?

The boy walked about outside his home in an agony of anxiety. Finally, he sent his young brother into the house to tell their father that he had swopped the cycle for three baby rabbits. He could not stand the suspense any longer.

Almost immediately, Fin appeared. With a black look in the direction of the boy, he strode around to the barn to confirm the loss of the bicycle. He must see the rabbits, already drooping in their cage. Fin reappeared and ordered the boy into the house. Inside, Fin spoke with a terrible quiet anger. He confirmed the facts, then said:

"You crazy fool! You have made yourself—and me!—the laughing stock of the whole village!"

The boy stood as always in front of his father, head down, waiting for the blow that would punish him and get it over. Fin was furiously angry, his pride deeply hurt. That a son of his could be so soft as to fall for a trick like this!

Martha watched them both. Silently.

The blows did not come. Instead, Fin told the boy:

"You will go straight down to White Sands and bring that bicycle back here. Do you hear?"

The boy trudged slowly, hopelessly, all the way to the next village. The lad was not at his home. At last the boy located him. He was leaning on the bridge at the bottom of the hill. There was no sign of the cycle.

"My father says you are to give back the bike."

The lad did not answer. He looked guilty, but the way he turned his head aside told the boy his plea was hopeless. Here was someone who was prepared to defy the power of Fin.

The boy went home and reported his failure. He received a contemptuous clout on the head that did nothing to assuage his anxiety and guilt.

Fin had decided to deal with the matter himself. The next day he singled out the lad from a group of schoolboys and bore down on him swiftly:

"You're the bird!" Fin told him. "You will return that bike at once, do you hear?"

The lad did not answer but after Fin had gone he and his friends mocked Fin's accent in the hearing of the boy. He did not return the bicycle and the boy heard that it fairly soon became a wreck.

The tiny rabbits were neglected in their prison. The boy was so sick at heart that he could not bear to go near them. He pushed some dock leaves through the bars once. But the rabbits were much too young to eat vegetation of any kind. They had been taken from the nest at too early an age; what they need was their mother's milk. One by one they died. Martha took the small stiff bodies one night when milking and buried them in the midden. Only the rusting bird-cage was left.

The current of the boy's life had slowed down for many weeks after this, until it was announced that he had passed his Qualifying and would go on to the town school.

Now, he stands outside the byre again, unwilling to enter it, fearful of what he may find. He can hear only the panting of the cattle, lying on over-full bellies, regurgitating, chewing, over and over. He *knows* that Fin, his father, is inside, probably in the barn, where the corn is to be stacked, beyond the grunting cattle in the byre. The boy is afraid.

It seemed to the boy impossible to open the door behind which his father . . . he had lately taken to swinging from the rafters of the barn since realising that all his friends were getting so much taller than he; the boy feared he was going to be stunted in some way and part of his secret life now included hanging from the rafters by his arms like an ape. He was secretly proud of the stunt, which he also hoped was helping his body to grow tall . . . he reached for the latch without realising he was doing it.

The door opened quietly. He stepped inside and closed it after him, holding the latch with both hands. There was nothing in the byre end but what he had expected to see; the steaming cattle lying in the green-stained straw; the empty potato hold awaiting its crop; the concrete dividing wall with the open door to the barn beyond. The hay was already gathered in and he could smell its sweetness; it had been a dry summer. Now the autumn had come.

The boy crept towards the opening. He could hear different breathing now, human breathing. He looked into the pale light of the barn. Fin was standing with his face against the wall.

His hands were clenched above his head. The boy watched the fists as, softly, they began to beat against the stones. No sound; only the breathing. Fin's head came back and he stared up through the low roof. The mouth opened wider, grasping for more air. No sound. Then, at last, a strange cry of pain:

"*O mo Dhette bheag bhochd.*"

The man's grief was not for himself. It was for the tiny child who had died when she might have lived.

As the boy turned away. Fin dropped suddenly to the floor; cut off at the knees he knelt in the hay.

The coffin was a small box covered in white material. It looked lost in the middle of the heavy black bier.

The boy thought it was a strange thing, that eight strong men should gather round to take it up and carry it away.

He stood by the end of the house, staring down at the black crêpe bandage on his sleeve. His father approached and laid a gentle hand on his shoulder:

"Come, my dear."

The boy burst into tears.

He knew that his grief was for himself, for what might have been, rather than for his parents or the pitiful child inside the wooden wedding cake.

The graveyard was by the sea behind the sand dunes, on the *machair*. The hole at his feet appeared deep and dry. The tiny coffin was lowered by the white ropes; it had no feel of weight at all as it bumped down to the floor of the sandy grave.

The ropes fell on to it with a hollow sound.

Perhaps it was already empty?

On Sunday, Fin put on his funeral suit and walked the three miles to the parish church in the next village.

# 7

# ANNE

Woolworth's store was the equivalent in the town of the public square in warmer climes. At certain times of the day, at lunchtime and between five and six in the evening, the warmth attracted into the store for a stroll around the counters just about everyone who was abroad on the streets of the town.

The store was especially popular with the country children at the secondary school whilst waiting for the bus to take them home. They felt themselves to be different to the sophisticated townies and were inclined to keep together.

The boy's friend at this time was called Barney and he came from a village on the other side of the island.

On an early summer afternoon in 1940, the boy and Barney were wandering around Woolworths together, looking at the perambulating people and at the displays.

There was a new parlour game on one counter; *Hang out your washing on the Siegfried line.* It did not interest them much.

They stopped at the sweet counter. It was not yet noticeably bare of confections, although there were rumours of rationing. It did not matter too much to them; they seldom had any money to spend on sweets in any case.

They stood and looked at the tempting coloured piles without resentment. Each was carrying a thick blue French reader under his arm.

A dark faced man in an ill-fitting grey suit suddenly bent over them:

"*Parlez vous Francais, hein?*"

The boy managed to gather his wits first.

"*Oui, un peu, Monsieur.*"

It was very exciting. The boys looked at one another. Barney's big nose was thrust forward as always when something caught his attention. *Good Old Barney*, thought the boy, affectionately.

The stranger was smoking a cigarette with an exciting foreign smell. He was waving his hands at the sales girl. Another man appeared silently beside them:

"Hello lads, met the Admiral have you?"

The Frenchman poured sweets into their hands.

The Englishman took his arm and they moved away.

"He told me to stick to French," said Barney, glumly chewing.

On the next day, they went down to the harbour and peered into the bay at the grey silhouettes of the ships that had left France behind in order to continue the war.

The Italian cafe was renamed the *Rendezvous* but the Frenchman went away.

The whey-faced woman teacher stepped towards the class, holding the sheaf of ink-stained papers.

"I have finished the marking."

She called a name and then another. The students went out and collected the papers, nervously, their eyes intent upon seeing the figure scrawled in pencil on the right hand corner of the top page of their papers.

The mark that would decide whether their school careers ended at fifteen or went on. The subject was mathematics; you needed a good mark in maths and English if you were to continue. And English was easier.

The boy also was nervous, but for a different reason. He dreaded the receipt of his paper because he *knew* it was a failure; a total failure. He had not been able to get beyond the second question in algebra; the incomprehensible formulae had filled him with a sort of despair.

Would he get any marks at all?

For months now, he had avoided the mathematics classes altogether. At three o'clock once or twice a week, he would walk with false confidence out of the gate, through the playgrounds of the junior school, and out into the street that led to the harbour.

At first, he had hidden in a cubicle of the fishermen's lavatories on the quay, reading to blot out the smell of stale beer, vomit and urine, laying a newspaper on the wet seat.

Then he became bolder and took to spending his time among the fishing boats, collecting the herring that fell from the baskets to take home or to sell for a few coppers.

One skipper invited him aboard. His hold was crammed with unsaleable herring; there was a glut. Tons of once bright fish lay in heaps open to the sky; their skins glazed grey in the afternoon, slow putrefying of guts had begun.

"Take as many as you want, son. There's a war on!"

The teacher had only a few papers left to distribute. His would certainly be last. Silently, she handed it to him.

He leaned over it to hide the mark from his companions.

Eight per cent, eight! He turned it over on his desk and stared at the bilious wall.

The teacher was speaking now!

"Believe it or not, one of you managed to get eight per cent in the Algebra paper; an astounding effort."

The boy did not move; he sat like a stone and stared at the Australia stain.

"One is evidently wasting one's time on such people. They are a waste of time and public money."

Holding his face tight, the boy turned his head the two inches necessary, carefully lowered his eyes and gazed into the sagging disappointed face.

"A waste of time and public money."

Their eyes met for an instant. Who looked away first?

At the least, Miss Drummond had not identified him by name. That would have been unbearable.

Would he have rushed out of the room?

He sat in the grey light and waited for the woman to appear on the screen again. The story of the film was forgotten; he wanted only to warm himself in contemplation of the cold beautiful face that held a promise of banked up fires.

What was her name? He must find out. The last scene faded without her. The lights came up to reveal the ramshackle plush seats.

Outside, in the pool of cold light that tried to keep the wet murk of the winter at bay, he scanned the pictures in the glass boxes. Who was this woman who had caught his excited attention? The garish photographs gave no final clue. He decided that her name was either Ingrid Bergman or Bette Davies but he could not be certain.

Whatever her name, he was deeply in love with her. Or was it love? He felt sad and at the same time was filled with a fearful excitement.

But it was good to have someone to share his thoughts with at least. She lay on a bed, as in the film and gazed *enigmatically* up at him. She made no demands, let him say whatever he liked. She was also completely inaccessible.

A few weeks later, he saw her in Woolworth's, standing pensively at the sweet counter. His stomach turned over and he felt his face go pale. The blood rushed back a few seconds later and he could feel it beat in his head. What if she saw him and recognised him? What on earth could he say to her?

In a rush of anxiety he stumbled across into the next aisle and stood staring at a display of hairnets. He could hear his own breathing now, deep and loud, like sighs. A girl in a brown smock was looking at him, her head to one side, examining him. He muttered something and moved away.

As his breathing became more natural, his anxiety took another direction. *I must brave it out.* Get it over. Just get it over and then he could relax. Relax!

He walked slowly back towards the sweet counter, threading his way among the dull oblivious men and women who strolled round and round in the warmth, waiting for the buses that would leave soon from up the street.

This was a time for action, for *braveness.* Was he not in love and are not lovers bold? A sudden panic; had she gone?

She was still standing where he had first seen her, calm and immobile. Her face was in profile and the cool purity of its beauty made his eyes smart. She turned towards him and saw him; the large grey eyes hooded themselves under huge lids.

She was holding a school satchel stuffed with books in front of her as she swayed towards him . . . Now she was close, passing him, and he spoke, naturally:

"Hello, Anne."

"Hello."

Her voice was husky.

She went on, and he let her go. He did not want to see her again for some time. To know of her existence was enough to bear at present.

Anne was the cousin of a friend, now transformed.

He went for the bus. The world about him was insubstantial. Only his thoughts were real. They consisted mostly of scraps of songs and music, repeating in his mind, like a stuck needle. He had found her and nothing else mattered for the moment. The time to tell was not yet. . .

"Three nine six! Jump to it!"

The squat man in the khaki suit bellowed again and he ran for the wooden hut. He was in, but it was unreal, like a film about someone starting his national service. When the NCO first shouted his name he did not move, it was all happening to someone else. It was February in Lancashire and the mud was everywhere between the big sad huts that looked ready to retire after their long war service. He had written and volunteered and waited until, at last, they had sent for him. He had wanted to get away.

In the third week the recruit with the foreign sounding name appeared to him in the ablutions, from the direction of the lavatories. His face was foolishly awry and he was holding a towel to his neck. He came up to him, leaning close, and mumbled:

"I tried to cut my throat."

He ran for the corporal and the man was marched away, around the square under escort, his cap off, the red towel jammed into place beneath his buttoned up greatcoat. Around the other side of the square strode the officer in charge. They met in the middle and all went into the orderly room. The sad one was charged with inflicting injury on himself. The official procedure was carried out to the letter. Only then did they take him to the medical hut. He was not seen again. Someone asked the hut corporal what would happen to him.

"He'll get two years."

He went into the strange city and he found the girls waiting. One of them took him on to some waste ground and told him softly in his ear about her father who was sleeping with her sister. He was not excited by her, not enough to overcome his shyness; her lipstick was thick and it tasted disagreeable. Alone in the pubs, he drank pints of the watery beer to get rid of it.

Back at the camp, he was good at some things. He contrived to come fifth, when he could have been second, in the cross-country race, anxious not to be noticed. To his surprise, he was timed first in his hut over the assault course and was matched with the other winners. To his relief, someone came up and asked him to step down in favour of an older man, who had spent the war in a factory and trained at the weekends. He did not want the limelight; but he got it on the day the CO found tea stains inside his mug, neatly upended on the clean inspection towel laid out on his barren bed. The hut corporal was bitter:

"You have lost us the Wing and probably the Flight as well."

Several of his mates looked at him accusingly.

"His mug full of the old bromide."

Towards the end of the eight weeks he was put for a day into the awkward squad.

"You look like a ruptured crab!"

*Needs chasing, that one.*

Someone found a turd in the showers. The Irish recruits in the next squadron were thought to be responsible. Two men from Glasgow asked him what his nationality was.

"I'm a Scotsman."

"Bluidy hell, hear whit he said Jock!"

He remained silent, his experience having already taught him that the islands of the north were unknown territory to mainlanders, whether Scots or English. From then on, when asked where he came from, he would reply simply:

"The Hebrides."

Sheep in Wellington boots.

# 8

# HINA

The sun blazed down on Wellington harbour and the dolls' houses that ringed the water showed no sign of life. It was a Saturday afternoon in January and nobody was at home who could go to the beach. Calum wiped the sweat from his eyes, went to the rail of the *Tui* and squatted in the shade of a lifeboat. He stared enviously at the twelve footers tilting at the harbour mouth as they searched for a breeze. He produced a tin and rolled a cigarette. The blue smoke he exhaled reminded him of the Lewis hills and the weary ache began again.

He studied the hairs on his left arm, bleached white by the sun and showing up vividly against the brown skin.

I could be pure Norse yet I think like a maudlin Celt. What kind of people are we—who travel the world yet never wanted to leave? What am I doing here far from *Eilean an Fhraoich?* Donald boy get yourself down to the Star tonight and fill your belly with *uisge beatha* and see if you feel any better. Or go and have a good—no, that's not the answer and you know it. Settle for the whisky—it's quicker and it's guaranteed to work.

"Dreaming again, you bastard!"

Calum leaped to his feet. The bosun was quite as tall as he and nearly twice as broad. His red eyes held memories of lunchtime beer and previous baitings.

All right, so 'bastard' is a term of endearment in the Antipodes. But this animal bears me no love.

He felt for the rail and braced against it. Ths bosun moved towards him.

"Finish chippin' that bulkhead?"

"No. Too damn hot to work."

"Should be glad you got a job! You Pommie jokers come out here and..."

"take your jobs, drink your beer and root your sheilas," Donald finished for him.

"That's right, matey. And less o' the lip and get that hammer goin'."

A spasm of rage shook him and he felt his lips stretch.

Taking orders is one thing but being abused by this ignorant slob is another. The worm turns.

"Fuck you Jack!" He spat the familiar epithet and immediately he felt better. Relaxing slightly, he repeated it. The bosun's jaw fell in surprise, thick lips gaping.

"You look like a bloody codfish!"

The bosun lurched forward and pinned him to the rail with one big hand. Calum knew fear and it smelled of beer and sweat. He writhed to get away but he was held like an insect on a board. A huge fist quivered inches from his mouth.

"Take that back! Take that back, you Pommie bastard or I'll smash your pretty face like a pumpkin!"

He daren't hit me more than his job is worth to hit me he's already got a bad discharge for grogging.

"Take it back!" The bosun rammed him against the rail.

Where's your Highland pride? Going to let yourself be pushed around by this illiterate spawn of a Sydney whore?

"Bannockburn, you Aussie Bastard!"

The big face creased in bewilderment.

"Eh—whass that?"

"Bannockburn!" Calum jerked his knee into the groin and felt it sink in beer flab. He plunged forward with his head and felt it crack into the bosun's face. The grip on his singlet relaxed and he dived to one side, his head ringing. He paused to gulp air and something struck the side of his head with stunning force.

The deck was so hot that it brought him round at once. His anger was gone and the fear came back.

Burned your boats this time jack and no mistake.

He got up slowly and moved his head to see if it was still securely attached to his body. He felt sad as he looked at the bosun, crouching warily a few feet away. He shook his head carefully at the big Australian and headed slowly for the ladder to the deck below. As he reached the bottom the bosun came to the top of the ladder and called down to him:

"Don't forget to pick up your meal money."

The old bastard! First time in two years he's called me anything but a Pommie this and that!

He came out into Lambton Quay to meet the traffic home to tea.

Everybody has a car and a load of brown kids. I've got a suitcase and a D.R. Decline to report we don't want to know you.

He dodged across to the railway station and put his bag in the left luggage.

He entered the cocktail bar of a five star hotel.

Very proud of their star ratings but they still turn off the taps in the public bars at six o'clock—just when a man wants a drink—or would if he hadn't been guzzling against the clock for an hour.

There was a carpet on the floor and the Guinness was ice cold. The barman remembered not to put a lump of ice in his whisky after the first time.

No barmaids allowed—too bad. Supposed to be very sympathetic—barmaids. No remarks yet about the plaster over the ear. Bash your face like a pumpkin. Your PRETTY face? He studied it in the mirror. Sorry Aussie—still got the looks but I take strong exception to the word pretty. What do you do now jack ashore? Ashore for good, too.

Have another, brother, before someone comes along and closes the bar. One good thing about N.Z. the booze is dirt cheap. Too bad they don't know how to treat it—or anything else. No wonder Katherine Mansfield took off—although she was homesick too, it seems. Are you homesick my fine plastered friend? Home is where the hat is but I've had a guts-full of Kiwi. Time to move on should have done it years ago but before I go I must pay my respects to my friends.

Come fill the flowing bowl my good and beerful servant and set up a dozen to carry out. It will be snowing in Lewis just now and the rollers will be streaming up Broad Bay like the Queen Mary in the Suez Canal. And a bottle of Black and White to prepare me for my return to the Isle of my heart.

> Isle of my dear, Isle of my heart
> Isle of my dear,
> Where I came apart.

But no islandman is complete in himself without his island and the water everywhere he looks. Be still you loud colonials and I'll croon for you the Eriskay Love Lilt and I'll sing for you Leaving Lismore and I'll cry for you baby the Isle of my Heart. . . but you have not the Gaelic and you have not the melancholy. You have nothing to cry for but the loser of the big race at Trentham and why did the All Blacks lose in South Africa. And it's a dry crying that. More's the pity for you're a fine bunch of fellows in a stoush. Time please—aye it's time right enough.

The party was in full swing when Calum and the girl entered the kitchen. He put the cardboard carton of beer and the bottle of whisky on an empty space by the sink. A brown face split across, showing perfect teeth, and brown fingers handed him a glass of beer. Hina disappeared into the other room, drawn by the music.

I hope there are no bloody pakehas here tonight I want to get drunk with my Maori mates.

"*Slainte,* Rangi!"

"*Kiaora!* I hear you got the sack!" Rangi roared with laughter and took his glass away. His hawk face showed his aristocratic ancestry, but Rangi was far from princelike in his attitudes.

You bloody beaut! That's what I want to hear! Laughter and singing and the throb of Island guitars. Some reckon that the Celts and Polynesians are two branches of the same tribe. One went West the other East and South. Maybe, but anyway I am at home with these people their joys are my joys and their sorrows my sorrows and they spring from the finest seamen in the world better even than the Norse. And the sun has kept them happy and the cold wet North has not seeped into their souls.

"How's the swot, Rangi?"

"Good, I take my Ticket in June."

"Will you pass, my old flower?"

"She'll be right, Cal—this time or next time, what's it matter, eh?"

That's the attitude Rangi boy that's the spirit. This time next time sometime never will you pass your exams and do you know why? Because you did not do as Rangi is doing and because you are a prize prick that's why. I wanted my own ship more than Rangi does, so what went wrong? Enough—ship's officers are two a penny. Jokers with D.R.'s are much harder to come by.

"Open the whisky, Rangi my brother and we'll drink to Peter Fraser."

"Good old Petey."

"Who's all here?"

"Just a few of the boys and a few more of the girls, Cal—you know them all."

"Extra *wahines*?"

"You already got a *wahine* boy."

"I'd better go in and see how she's going."

Hina was standing by the guitar player with her head thrown back and her arms rocked a cushion as she sang a Maori lullaby.

Be more than a cushion if you'd let me have my way. What charming supple hips my dear and what tight tits that never were tied down and the slope of your belly. I'm going to miss you anyway and what might have been if this country had been fit to live in.

Hina threw the cushion into the air; Calum caught it and she approached with undulating hips.

Amazing how they look innocent and erotic all at the same time.

He was aware again of the full lips, the even teeth and wide-spaced eyes. He gave the cushion to her with one hand and grabbed her round the waist with the other. She leaned complaisantly against him and rubbed her nose against his ear. He turned his face to kiss her and dropped the cushion to caress a pointing breast. She spun away with a laugh, her thick hair flying about her face.

What a laugh what a ripple of notes from the throat that is full of music. He had taught her a Gaelic song and she had picked up the melody in a few minutes.

"It is a sad song, Cal..."

"It is that."

"Like you, eh?"

"Don't be silly!"

He pushed towards her and as he reached her she slipped an arm through his and rested her head against him. She was unusually serious as she said:

"When are you sailing, Cal?"

"Tuesday at five thirty. The *Southern Cross*."

"Give my love to England—I mean Scotland!"

"Will you come to England—sometime?"

"Maybe—who knows? It is a long way."

"You don't sound very sure."

"I am not sure—I am not at all sure. I must go now and change for the poi dance." She slipped away from him into an adjoining bedroom.

He went towards the kitchen, to Rangi and the whisky...

He had not thought about Monica for years but she came back to him now in the dining room of the ship that was taking him home, as he studied the woman at the next table. Could it possibly—shaken, he remembered that Monica would now be forty.

He studied the fancy menu with one eye closed. The parting celebrations had been hectic and Hina had cried as she sang for him the haunting Maori farewell.

He had been moved then but now he felt a great surge of expectation. He could feel the beat of powerful engines quivering through the saloon and recklessly he waved to the wine waiter.

"Got any Scottish beer?"

"Youngers, sir?"

"We're on our way! Bring me a pint of Youngers!"

When you're eighteen a woman of thirty is very desirable when she is in her full bloom and wants it and knows it but when you're twenty-eight a woman of forty is an old bag—the same woman even. I wonder if she ever dumped that husband of hers. I wonder if the Bush Hotel is still snoozing at the end of the bush, miles from anywhere. Faretheewell dear Monica sweet spoiler of my youth!

"Two bottles in a pint glass, sir!" The waiter smiled his understanding as he slid the change under the cloth on his tray.

"Haven't seen a pint glass in years!"

"They don't use them, do they sir?" He jerked his head imperceptibly towards the stern.

"They do not. The glasses get smaller with every Budget."

Calum leaned towards him.

"Tell you something else, shipmate. They serve the beer from plastic hoses."

"Yes, sir—I had heard." The waiter looked pained.

"The standard of living is high, sir?"

"The money's good, if that's what you mean."

"Er, yes sir. Must excuse me, sir." The wine waiter swooped on a distant table.

Calum turned his attention to more solid food and was surprised to discover that the exotically named dishes were relatively tasteless. He chased a fleeting regret for crayfish and for steak, egg and chips with a glass of whisky and went up on deck and looked back over the boiling furrow astern.

> Tho' sailor I be
> I'm sick
> Of ploughing the sea...

A man should plough the land of his forefathers at some time in his life.

# 9

# CHRISTINA

Calum was uneasy. This was only his second visit to the Hebrideans since coming to London four years ago. Generally, he kept in contact with exiled island friends by meeting them in pubs in unlikely parts of the city. Pubs with familiar names on the bar pumps and unfamiliar tartan squares pasted on the walls.

He looked along the rows of disguised trestle tables towards the stage at the far end of the hall. On the shabby green curtains was pinned a huge white sheet with words "London Hebrideans—97th Annual Suipear" painted boldly in red.

"Salt herring, sir?"

He nodded and the waiter handed him a paper plate. On it lay two grey fish that visibly showed the effects of the long journey from the Minch to London. Calum smiled at the incongruity of being called "sir" when offered salt herring.

He looked around him and caught the eye of the woman sitting on his right. She smiled back and then looked away.

English, he thought, South Kensington written all over her. He studied her from the corner of his eye. Sleek dark head, fine-boned face, a Bahamas tan. Her firm throat had a single piece of jewellery placed between the double Venus lines and the plain black dress she wore had cost a lot of money.

He look around again, waiting for the potatoes to come. The hall was full; men and women sitting at long tables spread with cloths of coloured paper and laid with knives and forks. Despite himself, he resented the implied concession of the cutlery.

A waiter placed a large metal dish on the table. It was piled high with potatoes boiled in their skins. The woman turned to him:

"May I help you to a potato?"

Without waiting for his reply, she stretched out her left hand and prodded gently at the grey tubers. She selected one and placed it on his plate:

"Fingers only!"

Calum grinned at her and tried to think of something to say: unknown to him, his tongue was moving in his mouth to adjust to the polite English phrases he was thinking of and then discarding. His lips spoke involuntarily:

"The Hindus say food from the hand tastes better."

Her grey eyes looked straight into his. She looked down then, pulled a sliver of fish from the single herring on her plate and laid it carefully on the palm of her left hand.

"Why do the men get two herring and the women only one?"

"It's an old Gaelic tradition. A man is supposed to need more food." He laughed uncertainly.

She did not answer immediately. She placed the hand with the herring on it to her mouth and sucked up the strip of fish. She chewed it slowly, with small sounds.

"The Hindus are right."

She picked up a potato and pulled back the skin, bit off a piece and swallowed, then wiped her mouth with a paper napkin. Her eyes looked round at him again:

"There is no need to be so defensive about the eating habits of your people."

Calum squirmed inwardly but his face gave away nothing. I've done it again, what do the English want of me? Again he spoke from the back of his mind:

"The herring is a fascinating fish, really."

He thought about what he had said and was pleased with it. He found himself leaning towards her, because he knew that she was going to speak:

"What is so fascinating about the herring?"

"Their life is secret, like that of the salmon. They come and they go, nobody is sure where. And every three years..."

He paused.

"And every three years?"

Her eyes looked very big. He spoke again without thinking:

"Every three years they meet to mate at the bottom of the sea."

She turned away and stared ahead. Calum felt the familiar flush coming. Stupid heilanman's romantic rubbish. But she turned back to him, smiling:

"The salmon gets all the publicity."

Another waiter came past with a tray of white paper cups and placed one down for each of them. Whisky in paper cups.

Calum pretended not to notice his but she wiped her fingers, picked up her drink, and leaned towards him:

"What do you say?"

"Slainte."

"Slanje."

He picked up the yielding cup and tossed off the whisky. The smell of it mingled with the perfume she wore.

She sipped and turned back to the herring in front of her. Very carefully, she spread it open with her fingers.

It was an unspent female.

Calum's thoughts flashed back in time to his childhood and meals taken in the cottage on the island:

"You've got a roe!"

She took her fingers from the fish as though afraid of damaging it. Her hands hovered over the plate and she stared down at the firm mass of tiny flesh-coloured eggs.

"Eat it—go on, it's as good as caviare."

She shook her head and laid her hands in her lap.

"It's very good," he added uncertainly.

She made no reply but took a mouthful of whisky. Then she reached for the plate of oatcakes on the table and held it out to him:

"I'm sure you'd like one of these."

He took a piece and thanked her and told her of the bard on the island who baked his own oatcakes and refused to eat white bread.

She ate some oatcake and crowdie but the roe lay untouched on her plate and Calum looked at it greedily more than once. His own two herrings had yielded only slimy-soft grey male roes. Nobody eats them on the islands.

"Are the fishermen still superstitious?"

The sudden question startled him and he tried to think of a sensible reply. Images of men chattering in Gaelic on radio telephones, leaning against echo-sounders on the bridges of £50,000 trawlers, crowded into his mind. Was his cousin Angus superstitious?"

"Not now, I don't think," he said, and was aware of the lameness of his reply.

"Are there taboo words among them?"

"They used to refer to the salmon as the bald one. *Am fear Maol.*" She said nothing.

"It is the Gaelic for monk. Hence the name MacMillan."

"That means son of the monk?"

"Yes. And MacTaggart means son of the priest."

He waited for her to laugh but she did not. Instead she said:

"It was a healthy society in the old days."

They were silent. The waiter took away the crumpled paper plates with their mess of fish bones and potato peelings and put cups of tea on the table. The tea was fresh-made and Calum was relieved to see it was served in real teacups. She turned to him again:

"Do the people retain the second sight?"

He was thrown off balance once more by her sudden question and pondered what to say. Calum was glad that nobody he knew was sitting near to him. At last, he told her, cautiously, of the most recent case of second sight in the islands that he had heard about.

"Do you believe it?" Her eyes were intent on his face and again he replied without thinking:

"Why should the woman lie about such a dreadful experience?"

"But there are happy experiences surely, associated with second sight."

"You must allow for the psychology of the people."

Calum was pleased he'd said that. What a stimulating companion she was!

But what *was* the psychology of the people? What people? Who are the people with all this psychology? His sudden happiness now gave way to confusion and he realised her face was very close to his. The light caught the object on her throat, half cross, half teardrop.

"What is your name?" he asked.

"My name is not important."

"Mine is Calum and it is not important." He found himself giggling and her face drew away. He blinked and said:

"Let's go back to the pub."

"I haven't been to the pub. But I shall come with you."

In the sidestreet leading to the pub they passed a kilted figure with its face pressed up against the basement railings. From the folds of the kilt rose a hot stream that arced between two bars and fell into the darkness below like a rain storm.

Calum was angry and ashamed and he hurried her past. He heard a low sound from her throat and feared she would speak, and she did so:

"Why don't *you* wear a kilt?"

"We leave that to the romantics!"

"Who is we?"

"The islanders. My ancestors would have found a kilt of damn little use in an open fishing boat on a dirty winter's night! They wore trousers instead." He pushed open the door of the saloon bar.

The pub was crammed with excited people who had not seen each other for months. Calum could tell at a glance they were nearly all highlanders. Their aura of self-confidence in the strange mileu stimulated him and he turned to smile at his companion with unspoken pride.

She was standing beside him, very still, listening intently to a group of men and women singing a mournful Gaelic song.

He saw a table in a quiet corner and drew her towards it. At the next table sat a solitary London family, bemused by the alien atmosphere suddenly imported into their local. A middle-aged man in the party called out to him:

"Where are the pipers, mate?"

Calum pointed vaguely out of the window in the direction of the hall. The man rose and stood over them:

"I want to hear the pipes playing," he said, and leaning over them confidentially:

"I was at Alamein with the Jocks." He blinked at them.

An old woman at the next table called out in a London voice and the ex-soldier went away. The cockney woman began to sing "Knees up Mother Brown," striking the table in time to the tune.

She gave up after a few lines as the Gaelic song swelled to its climax.

Calum's companion let out a pent-up breath as the song ended and he watched her now become fully aware of her surroundings. He moved closer on the seat and was surprised to find his hand gripping her knee. Her flesh was hot and firm and his palm slid easily along the smooth nylon.

She turned to him with an expression he had not seen before, a direct challenge. What a wicked look, thought Calum, I wish I'd had a few more whiskies. His hand fell away from her, pushed off by the aura that excited and scared him at the same time. She seemed to sigh before she spoke.

"I could feel the yearning in that song."

"You're right," replied Calum and waited.

"It was the male yearning to possess the female."

Calum stared at her in embarrassment but managed to say:

"You understand Gaelic!"

"Translate it for me," she ordered.

He stifled the resentment he always felt at the assumption he had met so often, that he could give instant translations of Gaelic subtleties. He tried to answer her as well as he could, desperate to regain favour in the eyes of this intoxicating stranger:

"A fisherman is back from sea in the early hours and he lies beside his wife in the bed, telling her of what he saw and what he did and what he thought. In the refrain, he keeps saying to her—'Put away sleep and turn to me'."

"That is not bad."

"Where did you learn Gaelic?" said Calum with quick cunning.

"What do you know of the old religion?" she countered.

"What do you mean?" he forced himself to say. His mouth had dried up.

"Simply that. The old religion."

Calum felt cold. He thought of the tales his grandmother had told him. Tales of strangers who travelled at night on dark errands.

There was a pause that went on so long Calum felt forced to do something to break it. She was smiling at him, out of her still face. He knew he had to say it:

"You mean—black magic?"

"Magic, yes—but not necessarily black."

He drew a deep breath and his thoughts whirled. He plucked a word from them and threw it at her:

"*Buisneachd.* Witchcraft."

She nodded at him: gentle and understanding, reminding him forcibly of his mother. How old *was* she, for God's sake?

She leaned closer and stretched out her right hand to him with a terrible slowness. He stared in horror at the spread fingers approaching his face. Before they touched him, her left hand came forward and fell on his thigh. A cold shock sprang to his centre.

He jumped to his feet, mumbling words, and hurried away from her. In the toilet, he locked himself in the little cubicle and sat trembling on the black seat.

After a time he began to read the grafitti scrawled on the back of the door. One caught his eye and held it: the name of a famous pop singer.

Next to it were the words:

"He wears his mum's knickers."

He leaned back against the hard pipe, closed his eyes and listened to water hissing in the urinal. His mind drifted off and he saw himself swimming in warm water.

He went along effortlessly gliding but he knew he had to go deeper where the water was darker and as he turned down into the purple depths he saw the white shadow and he aimed for it and as he came deeper and closer he could see her waiting for him but he had to go still deeper to meld himself into her. Now he became aware of the life around him as millions of fish-like forms crowded about him and it seemed to him they were all aiming for the white body below that he claimed for his own and he began to struggle against the ever more closely pressing mass of movement about him that threatened him.

A door slammed and aroused him and he got to his feet and went back upstairs, hoping she would be gone. Yet very anxious to know her.

The pub was empty apart from the last to leave, the groups in corners, collecting partners and carry-outs for the parties.

She had gone from the table and a terrible sense of loss flooded him. He saw a fur cape by the door, recognised the proud head above it and ran to her:

"Wait for me, please wait for me!"

She turned a blank face to him and shook her head, pulling the fur around her throat, touching the jewel there.

He caught her shoulder and then dropped his hand when he saw her face still closed to him. He knew it was no use.

"I have a car waiting," she said, "Goodnight."

She went outside and crossed to the kerb. A black clad chauffeur was holding open the door of a long black car. The woman settled herself in the rear seat and he shut the door and walked around and got into the driving seat.

A tall grey-haired man in a kilt stepped past Calum and waved at the car, calling out confusing words in Gaelic. A hand fluttered in the rear window as the car surged away.

As the man in the kilt turned, Calum stood in front of him and demanded:

"Who was that woman?"

The man frowned, shrugged and decided to answer:

"Christina. She's on the committee."

"Christina?"

"Aye. She belongs to Uist."

He pushed past Calum and went inside.

# 10

# HELEN

You draw down the lamp to illuminate the bare sheet in the machine Helen writes in ink on large yellow sheets you asked for yellow sheets on the new firm-edge double bed and last night you like this corner you can see the cement mark where they filled in the hole left in the floor when they removed the pedestal Helen said What colour sheets love and you said Yellow for our incestuous sheets and she said Corny but not so black tiles on the floor a new conversion you can see the wall tiles outlined through the red wallpaper that has split like a prim mouth where you ran your finger speak or forever hold your piece you could write a bedsitter novel or Helen and her heilanman on her back in a cave in the islands and the pebbles staining her skin with pink bruises the novel is dead long live the when did the possibility of you ending up in Islington writing a novel because the cowed boy rejected because you could not hiding in the lavatory on the pier that first time for the full hour of the maths lesson in case someone skulking they called it the Calvinist equivalent of playing truant the English name all things with moderation and now you are among them accepted by a Maybe you can tell you must help me Tod we shall help each other to your problem may not be your father I love you darling and I want to help you so that both of us when I was six I lay in bed in the room with my sister and I listened to mummy and daddy next door their bed was by the wall and I heard the terrible sounds the wall receded and my legs and arms and fingers grew and swelled as I heard the noises behind the wall that went away and came back and the room swelled and my limbs swelled and contracted faster and faster until the sounds stopped darling Tod you must help me and I shall help you to It was in the local paper Boy Steals Key From Old Lady's Cottage Is Punished by Angry Headmaster Father Withdraws His Support Perjured Evidence Admitted at School Trial Village Lad Marked For Life Mother Fails to Understand He will always piss the bed now Helen was wearing the suit you like best the one that enhaunches her height and shows off the elegant legs she was smiling and leaning over you and her hands were on your hair the fingers so long and so supple she read His mother smelled her fingers after she had gutted the herrings darling you are obsessed with fishy smells and roes Roes by any other name very sexy are fishy smells how was today Not bad read a marvellous serial about the Russian Revolution the woman has captured the whole atmosphere of pre-revolutionary you did not speak then feeling her hands on the back of your neck the thin hair her hands brushing the hair upwards you felt the prickle of you turned your head and strained up to her and twisted around in your chair and raised your hand to her face she held your hand to her face and dropped it and you slapped her rump and she smiled gratefully Want a drink My name is Tod and I'm an alcoholic You could not help it you are a sick man Tod you must learn to forgive yourself we are all sick we are not responsible for the terrible things we God Grant Me The Serenity To Accept He went into the house and sold a lot of insurance after seven years he was so successful and he took one glass of sherry and a few months later he was dead pleading For God's sake stop me drinking please stop me but we could not you have to do it yourself This Is a Do It Yourself Programme but who is to blame for who is responsible My name is Tod and I am Darling I want to help you must tell me your dreams last night I was back at the college and having an affair without telling you and I went into the lavatory and locked the door and started I felt cold and the door opened as though I had not locked it at all and in came the woman who had come to take me away to she was black and beautiful Indian or African dark with my mother's when she was I woke up screaming Why Why Why and you took my hand I woke up screaming and you were fast asleep the night before last a man was pinned between two trains speeding along between the windows right next to me I pulled the cord and his body fell into a hole by the track a redirected letter Please Forward If Necessary Helen hands it to you as you open a woman's hand on the envelope two womens' she stands over you thinking Mother and the last girl both knew him before you open it and read bits to her Taken a new job away from the place where we hope to see you sometime Helen I have told you about her we never made it she was too poetic justice you pick up her Virginia Woolf and find the sheets typed tight Helen looks at you with glee I wrote this after the first time I made love with a man it is a good piece of writing I don't want to read it tit for but not so she made it and you did not the jealous skin crawls with the fear Shall we go straight to sleep Get ready you want to prove you work on her with a hand that is not too gentle like you did with and she has her then she mounts and crouches she takes over her haunches swinging I love this sometimes her face lit with the power of it her fluid hips the sliding and drawing takes you over she needs this to arm her against the powerful rutting bitches that haunt her and send her to stand in the corner a little girl that cannot ride with a man bigger than daddy a hard run mare her face but you do not let her you grip her hips and take over a man's superior do not let her hold her and hold her using the only the bone on her bone faster and faster and she calls out and she is yours as she cries out over the creak Did you come too Yes The book is about what is happening now to you and to me a diary of mental events only what is inside the head is real all is fiction how do you get inside Helen's head Helen's Dream 10th July I was showing my parents the new flat, it had blue wallpaper but in the middle of the floor there was a huge family tomb in caramel-coloured marble veined with pillars and a canopy of marble and on the raised plinth there were four effigies they were my mother and my father and your mother and you and inscribed round your effigy were the words To My Son daddy and I were agreed that we'd have to get rid of this but I said that the tomb could not be razed completely because the ground would be consecrated and holy but what I could do was to take away the whole marble structure re-bury the bodies under the floor and put a little brass plaque to mark the spot in the shape of a fleur de lys I saw it quite clearly with a long central tongue and the two curved leaves on each side above the tomb in the same caramel-coloured marble were thin delicate flights of stairs straight out of a TV programme on Leonardo da Vinci these stairs led up to a magnificent organ also in marble daddy and I agreed this was a wonderful acquisition I tried to persuade daddy to come up and play the organ since he used to be very good at it but halfway up the stairs he insisted on turning back saying I don't want to play I'm no good any more I thought it was wonderful to have the organ in my flat and I thought of the marvellous times when alone I would sit and play it and make wonderful tunes on it Saturday in Soho Helen said I want a drink and suddenly you wanted one too and you went at once to a wine shop and bought the bottles and you both rushed back to the flat and you drank and drank

The swallowing and the release and the warmth and the talk talk talk

On Monday the black reality inside and out

I must stop

After the drinking it is the one way to release the terrible tension that makes your body scream for more and today I must stop I Helen please look at me holding it is the one way to stop the

You survive

Tod's Afternoon Dream College . . . a huge tower, a tower dreamed of previously, with an elaborate tunnel system for "escape". And also for the lowering down to the earth of the coffins of the dead from the Abbey Chapel where the old monk's skull is kept on the wall in a cardboard box.

In the college is Helen—and others. We seem to be distant. I go to the canteen/bar place and save a table for Helen and the others. Nobody turns up.

Instead, there is a meeting of students. Before the meeting starts, I stand up and say, in Gaelic;

*"Tha Ian thide an canan so a bhi air a chluinntinn ann a so."*

Immediately, several students stand up, identifying themselves as Gaels or supporters of Gaelic culture.

One of the students pushes an elaborate Application Form for a Society of Gaels into my hand. He is an American, I think. But we are prevented, after some words about Rules and Procedure, from going on with our Gaelic meeting.

(I have been aware of a death, a funeral to take place in the college) As we leave the meeting, the cortège bearing the flower-strewn coffin is being borne into the chapel, from which it will be sent down below through the elaborate tunnels (now worked by machinery) in my dream. "Sssh!" I say to the chattering students. "A funeral!" Behind me, students laugh and push me, including a girl near me who looks like Joan, Helen's sister, dark where Helen is fair.

I go down to the ground, outside, and look up at the huge fortress-like building of the "college".

The "funeral" wheels and ropes (wire) on the side of the tower are moving slowly, indicating that the coffin is being lowered through the tunnels.

In the entrance to the "college" I meet and have some words with some roughs and then I go to my new dormitory.

It is very untidy, crowded and unsatisfactory.

I wonder why we have been moved from our nice wee private single rooms. Sean Smith, the playwright, is also there, preparing his bed. Tod darling I like the story of the seaboots but you said you were writing for the two What about what I said about the difference between writing a book for one or writing for I think you have gone a lot further than I have Tod You mean what the book is about For me it is the relationship Is that because it is more simple for me writing a book and not The thing is Tod your focus is on the novel my focus I don't really know where my and this is why I need to be very much involved in the relationship up till now all my efforts have been on making my own life and separating from family and making my own and having I want to do something different if its really two people doing their own just happening to be in the same place at the same time having a certain type of commerce then I'm just as I was before in a worse position I'd rather be absolutely alone. *The book is everything*

And I and I just have to feel really really that the relationship has a real identity for me to be completely taken into it

*The book is you all is the book      Helen*

Did what I said at the beginning about the importance of the fact of there being two people in the book writing the book almost instead of the usual existentialist one did this make it any better when I told you I was trying to get at you through the novel It made me feel tremendously better that you talked you know you won't meet me through the novel you will meet you through the novel you won't meet me you will meet you Tod you won't meet me you'll meet you and you'll meet your feeling about me.

*You bastard you cannot communicate with*

You won't meet me in the novel Is that enough all that is possible it is not possible for me to meet you through the novel No It is only possible for me to meet my feelings about you through the is that enough does it satisfy No it does not satisfy unless outside the novel you do want to meet me

*I have never met anyone*

Well yes I do of course I do Helen that is one of the reasons for writing the

*Your laughter is uneasy*

On the face of it could look very selfish but I tried to say then we started that I was trying to meet me and then having found out me I would thereby find

*Did you say that did you say*

Be able to come out to you Yes that yes yes And the whole thing is all tied up in there are so many things there is the need to sort oneself out Yes There is the need to write the novel Yes I mean it is a need and the need to order the material wildly floating about in one's and in one's life with you at this moment in time and to bring them together and to put them into some sort of order would never be attempted if I did not have the compulsion to write I have got the two things together I have not deliberately sat down and it just happened that way Yes yes no I am not attacking at all But are you jealous of the novel in spite of you are making it possible If I discover if it becomes to seem that I am being used for the novel and for you and that is really the extent of my then it will not No I would not expect it to be no it is a very complicated situation it could happen that you would begin to suspect that Yes But you do not suspect it No no I do not I do not

*Thank God*

When you talked to me about yourself Tod then I hoped that that is
important
*How you feel*
It is vital I never met anyone yet ever there is no-one in my life never
has there been and no sign of who ever would have the interest the
intelligence the feeling to enable me to find myself through it just is
not possible without you find myself through it is just not possible
without it is not just that you are someone that one is using for the
novel there just is not anyone else in the entire world and I cannot
conceive of there being anyone else love and you must Yes yes and
you must look at that I do I do I do
*Now you laugh easily*
You must I do not ask you to forgive me Tod that is the way I am but
I do have these dreadful feelings of inadequacy not knowing I do not
really yet know where I will know Yes you will know I will know
we'll both know and although it is my novel but possible only
through you and your help and support and love and encouragement
and everything absolutely would not be possible and it is a vital a
vital thing for me this novel for so many reasons it is not just an
expression of and it is my whole life is involved in this thing Yes yes I
know So you can see that you are just as important to me as the
*You are embarrassed you laugh*
Yes yes And I am I will not say confused but I am working out both
Yes yes It is very difficult and from the outside it could look like
manipulation but it is not because I keep saying it is not
*What are you saying*
I mean it is not because I keep saying it is not I have tried to explain
why it is not Oh I know it is not and I believe it is not and I think you
put upon me this feeling of jealousy of the novel which is not actually
Good good All I am concerned about is getting enough of you and in
a sense a person is not divided whether the novel is there or not the
kind of things one wants from a person are limitless if they are to be
given and the novel does not come anywhere between them in any It
must not if it starts coming between us then it is not working
*You are speaking sense*
No Not working the way it is supposed to work
*You both laugh with relief*

In a way the novel is a safeguard
*She is doubtful*
I mean how many girls get a running diary of waved at them when they come home at night have a look at this
*She giggles*
How many girls would have the patience and understanding The thing for me is whether I can make a life and that is what it is all about for me and for you Tod it is whether you can make the novel Yes yes that puts it in a nutshell it has possibilities and It is It is exciting and different and the possibilities It is At other times one feels it is a bit funny and it is not what usually
*You both laugh you giggle together*
Last night you were it did not work for Helen asked if she turned you felt the ease of the rider for the first as you swayed back and fro back and fro it began to work you loved her Oh yes yes yes you were in her back working for both Punish me for punish me Tod and after English cannot the great language has no words for Piss off epic poetry was in Gaelic before Anglo and Saxon ever piss off Helen you were bold scared but He is talking to me is that what she then you slept not the night before sitting looking at her story scattered on the floor barring the way to your desk her desk You do not work very hard Tod punish me darling foolscap sheets in the hot early morning no sound the papers on the floor now the chink chink of a hammer a mason chinks in the hot dawn another conversion a workman works you do not another cigarette looking later at houses with her sister posh town and rotten victorian she was happy the children calling Helen abandoned the desk to you was it the play made her ask I have a good body the naked women jerking with spread legs jumping paps that do not belong only the black girl was the fair one with cream breasts half-hard like her clumsy fillies you want to ride them not the knowing dark ones Yes you have beautiful legs back arms not bad breasts better than most of the Bacchae they need milk to fill you did not say can the fair ones have the power of the dark maybe deeper England was Finding out bodies hers sensitive to stroking at the base of you stroked each other in the unfamiliar place and you talked instead of If only we had more time Tod crowding the most important part of our Sell the television and buy a new Someone has

to work Tod while did you feel guilty it did not work for her in spite You always come Tod but Women are so complex love exciting deeper do you think the dark ones the fair ones have to work so much harder she did and her determinipples caressing your chest hair the damp fury of her using you I'll die if I don't come dont come dont you let her strive the first time ever a bacchante in your bed true mystery you rise now to think twice she rested then attacked and on the third time You've never let yourself go like Is it bad when I am selfish you said that Beatrice She turned her back once before Helen bears she broke her bond and used you for her own the first time she forgot and went inside herself the dark came out and took her over the hidden power of the fair female so deep the sexual strivings of blondes obscene as though not entitled to groan teeth and thighs gripping agony for them not pleasure as for the dark ones who take their pleasure as it comes so easy thank god for puritanism this morning she put her hair up for the first time you watched her from the bed the prickle you ran to her crushed her against your she laughed It is because I remind you of your surge of feelings in your I will be all right now the pressure goes with a last inner I'm off darling see you tonight but now it comes back and you hold yourself now men have killed themselves then they become impotent others have not I don't care if I do go blind do go blind do go blind Sean and his lady wife after the weekend writing course what a madness locked himself in the kitchen for six months to finish the novel of the Belfast priest copies done on the firm's machine a true patriot but not yet of the family of Daedalus The first thing to entertain the poetry will out if I read Malone three times and end with the same word christ a man dying locked in a lavatory one breath left to use all the words in new ways like on my own page they go too far He is a philosopher cannot separate thinking from reality all that is real is the mind in chaos you cannot return to the 19th century truth inside your head form to the inner man content Who wants to read it Who indeed outside a black cat squirts his city mess on the patch of green with elegant rhythmic thighs you think of the texture and firmness of country last night after Sean and Cathleen you asked her What is the matter but she would not you kept on and Helen said They are so right for each other are we Because I am a crofter and you Yes you

use bad language Tod in front of Only one four-letter word I was
excited You eat too fast I sat on the right of daddy every time I did
something he clipped me I was taught one mouthful talk and drink
but you what will people I do not give a damn what people Jimmy
Porter and Alison twenty years later on for I try love pour the wine
and wash for all but the middle classes eating is just the upper classes
eat like pigs that is the joke on Mummy and Daddy are coming for
lunch I think they have got used to the idea of us Love I cannot dine
in the way to which you have been accustomed on apple juice later
no cigarettes she smoked them you go out into the midnight streets
no machines Vandals smash em up sir a pale girl in a purple scrap of
skirt is bailed up against a patrol car In Need Of Care and Protection
Helen comes looking for you in her nightgown I thought it would be
taken for an evening dress startling metamorphosis of the emcee
female yet who else would you sleep badly dream of looking for her
in a camp a sergeant in a blue suit says We only do twenty working
dramas we cannot use then you fail with a virginal dark female in an
open barracks And you sniff a lot o god Tod why should I want to
change you Specially as I am always picking your pants up off the
floor She wanted you to go to college although After finals I had a
bottle of champagne on the lawns from daddy we went on the river
it was the most wonderful wearing a carnation on her gown the men
in morning suits to sit in the photograph five hundred years of
history looming why did she become unhappy why do so many of
them suffer the segregation you told her you felt exhausted after
three weeks of no place to be alone The first time for twenty years I
must tell you though you may hate No darling we must speak of we
are alike in many When you nuzzle up to me Helen I feel responsible
for your But you must not Tod I am strong we are free and if it
does not work nobody is going to I shall not die Four pm Saturday—(afternoons best for noting dreams Have just woken from
a very heavy afternoon sleep—fairly short, about one hour). It
was as though coming up from drugs or something. I had to drag my
fingers apart and twist my head around desperately, in order to
awaken myself.
Two short dreams. Something before—party? no drinking; college.
*ONE*

In my room somethere or other and waking up to find a drunken party going on. I try to evict "Clockwork Orange" type thugs. This creates a certain amount of unpleasant trouble but no serious consequences, that I can remember. Although there were some young "scrubber" type girls present also, there was a covertly homosexual aura about some of the young thugs.

It was very unnatural.

I think I got them to leave at last.

*TWO* (Later?)

Outside my room, I have a MS(?) Picture(?) in my hand. I feel very happy and free.

I come to a huge old/new hall, with curving beautiful circular walls and mirrors of indescribable shapes, not natural, of differing heights and perspectives.

I dance around in a "high"—natural, not drugged, delirious at such curving, altering beauty in this big hall/room.

A student takes me by the arms and says:

"Fine baby, but not so near the church."

Around the corner, as another part of the huge "college" building I am now aware of the dark, brooding interior of an old church.

I cease to dance, and go about my "business", whatever it was. On Sunday afternoon with the curtains time to talk as well The Europeans are civilised every afternoon Darling Tod I feel confirmed can one approach God through there are no doubts after I have but you know they will come back in Lewis a strange fisherman enters the cottage and says to the girl I have come for you and she says But I got my advance today for the herring gutting and he says What do you want me or the herring and she hangs her head I want thee and they lived happily until he was now there is no simplicity we want to be the same but our needs Is there richness or poverty for us in our different Oh richness Tod richness two cultures One and a half more like does she believe deep down you want to believe is it the usual sellout crying in their whisky in Detroit Melbourne London a few go home to die in concrete bungalows What happened to the wonderful life we left now you have running water and gee the wonderful people all gone all I see are goddam visitors and trailer parks in the garden leans the witches broom against the sooty wall you move it two frantic spiders Stein says they represent the devouring mother yet most of her friends are women Beatrice feared snakes yet most of her friends were men she had a lot before you turning herself into an object Helen wont go into the Greek shop now the man made a pass his wife away at a funeral She hates me I can feel it But how could she know you go for a walk before Youve been chatting up that blonde Have I hell your anger is based in truth this time I may be to do with my fear of women All My Best Friends Are Sean rings before breakfast Thank you for useful crit I must do more work on Your problems is point of view you must be consistent choose first or third then But I thought I had got away with You are writing a conventional novel Sean and must abide by the you must learn the rules before you can see they must be there are no rules but the reader has certain expectations learned But I have pieces of stream of consciousness Later Sean the apprenticeship comes first who the hell are you to Helen does not speak listens and says nothing goes off to edit thinking You arrogant pig who the hell are you to advise was she thinking or was she jealous of you feel desperate the novel depends on her You open painful eyes you feel Helen's hand in the dark light throws patterns on your neck is tight pain between the eyes You were crying in your sleep Tod like a baby This afternoon I tried to go back to the key why I was ready to accept Helen I walked the streets yesterday no words came for the useless You must not equate the novel with anything lesser darling guilt is something we both must Helen I stood by the wall in the playground during the inquisition I was not worthy for one bigger boy braved the waves of Admit you stole the key and he will let you go there were others in front of the head eliminating them one by one he left me to last framed by the boy who got my prize his mother and our teacher Helen something happened before the dreadful or why did I admit a lie such a small boy it is nothing when you think it ruled your life your father thought you a thief went to town and bought a new lock for the old woman Take that back to replace the one you did away with everybody thinking you guilty even you knew nothing the informer said he saw but your father proved he could not from why did he not tell the headmaster you were left alone you said I did it I did it let me go let me be all happy the case solved Put the file away its now opening up in your head why should a Something happened to you before the key that made you darling Tod maybe you never resolved the oedipal aggression we must not be afraid of her face shuts What the hell is wrong with Nothing Tod may I not be quiet without you feeling it is you are relieved you shouted she accepted a pillow fight at midnight she swings clumsy child's face angry with you feint and hit her hard you laugh to hysteria she hits you do not make love after she laughs This evening Friday relaxation she says Tod you are a different person when you open out excited by her mind a mouthful of white wine This is the stuff I shall drink when I go on the urge to take more sweets stop you open out without There is a side of me Tod wants freedom money travel social work instead of What about a woman must have children on their own You can get a brood mare from the islands but you must marry women can have children alone men must marry to So women are freer than men have pressures to conform too when in Lewis the first thing my brother Is it not time for you to settle maybe he is no encouragement Helen without you too much despair maybe another book later the two of us alternate chapters there is no absolute truth all is fiction the present is the nearest you can before the mind tonight dress up for does it excite Yes it opens me to you tell her about whores in Panama Port of Spain to but she says I feel absolutely turned off you both try hard she works better than Good girl good girl good girl she hates and fails with both Do not call me your little girl I am not a child's face angry but later One comes simply if one wants she sleeps and Tod I dreamed my friend Alice and I were watching a play you were in it we sat in the third row back below the stage I think the play was Hamlet you were Hamlet dressed entirely in white velvet you had white velvet shoes rosettes white velvet hose short white velvet Elizabethan breeches a white velvet doublet a white velvet cap with a white feather after the play I wanted to be with you were full of your performance very ebullient there were lots of girls from the cast you had no time for me when I wanted to talk you were angry at my interference Alice and I left the theatre walked down a cold dark street it was raining to where Alice's mother was waiting in a black Morris Eight my grandparent's car I am very fond of Alice's mother white hair round face blue eyes always smiling and loving she had presents for us to give to Hamlet a red box of chocolates for Alice to give for me a red box and a much larger gold box I was very confused I knew morally the gold box was for me that it was very important I should keep it and not give it because it would be childish to give it what I must do is keep the gold box to myself give the red box to Hamlet that was the right and balanced thing to but I needed to give both boxes to Hamlet then I would be at peace but I know that was wrong in the end I decided to keep both boxes Tod I dream in vivid colours when menstruating bright blood only greys when we were decorating on high ladders mine was just as high as you hand me an instrument at the match her first time high in the mass behind a goal a unit of the pack trying to bay with them and not I was frightened Tod could not breathe *You'll never walk alone* the roar in the blood *Shit shit shit* pity and terror from the mob not the players did they start her flow Suicidal tension and despair sometimes Have a drink have another Canute trying to stem the tide guilty because they have wasted another egg millions more your blood rises to meet her release comes from outside blue sheets a roar in the dark and the rain flushing down using herself like a secret hand pinioned underneath her rise and fall the exquisite half drawn and covered half drawn and covered the tide creeps from your toes to near break and fall back near break and fall back you can stand it and you can not pinned below the powerful female one who ministers with love and power forgetful of Helen in charge of her careful hips the joy on her as she gives and gives and gives taking your nerves to life from feet to calves to thighs to centre to centre to blinding centre you cry out to her twist to get away to get more you must have you cannot stand it You are killing me Helen I am reborn outside the prisoned puppy wails for his mother Hollywood truck driver symbols not polished men in sports you wait in the shop the dark girls knowing eyes when he comes in her spread buttocks always leave the door open stopping jumping down in one smooth hairy chest her underarms they both know Do you mind a woman laughs her purse tight she buys an icecream for her son Tod you must not drink if I shall not mother approves but does Helen Love it is playing with fire you have some alcohol you are responsible you choose telling her what she both relaxed quiet bar anonymous lovers You mother me Tod rocking to the lullaby it is the movement of the womb *oh an oh an oh an oh gheibh i caorich gheibh i cro* father was hard when I drank it was him in me who punished maybe stopping after he died and was saved Maybe Tod I am your mother now her rubber spider squeaks and leaps on a swelling red stalk Helen I love my father ran away to New Zealand still looking a prize from the officer a bribe to sign away my free first woman there in the playground by the dark hotel she bore me her grip wombsoft her smell he saw me brush the dried juice from my Darling Tod you may be looking for mother still when I am maybe we shall grow out of the needs now you do not speak the need for being alone leaps a rubber spider now you need her for the book needs Helen we are together it is good feeling the objects in the gallery Groping blindly Helen on your desk you do not understand her strange blind place she knows you better but she is hungry you must feed Helen love please get ready randy both afraid of a third she wants immortality also Darling Tod saved from setting sail for Lesbos by a kiltie on a white charger wearing a white blouse breasts sagged crumpled skirt bulged with indulgent hips aware eyes in a beautiful face watch you mere man I can give her more pleasure in half an hour than you can in half a lifetime you talked to her about the film maybe Chabrol is just making a gangster film stop playing hunt the symbol you fought her better than a man later Helen going with her how can you be jealous of a no-prick you thought H was taunting you with the ambivalence of the femme most woman are bi-sexual I feel sorry for her Tod she is my friend You are terrified Helen yet you Only supper there is nothing never has the thought makes One day you will know your own mind she said before we met Tod I cannot just stop Treat her like a man who made a pass and failed to tell her to buzz off and leave Darling its over now about us together could London the island two homes all my friends There are people in the islands with similar because all your friends came through trouble are you never going to make two years enough maybe we could But what about children bad for Schooling there is better than more graduates per head Yes it is a good life but all my friends You are happy with her drinking dangerously If nothing after life is absurd an optimust commune on the scrubbed benches rare simplicity no

hunger rare generosity you walk home together through spread drops to the best supper Helen I will give the land to my brother so he may build reckless with love she is silent now closed you probe It is revolting Tod revolting the powerful woman this week her strong perfume sitting by her to learn how you try to cope with the return of that you thought over a mere male staff of blood they do not what can you helpless to ignore a proud with lipless mouth she says When I am like this I hate men you say nothing you say nothing silent the darts hiss into the board a woman stretches a glimpse of breast with rubber tip would she let you or her or anyone opposite three boys in denim ignore three girls who drink from their glasses treats em rough well harrowed and poorly shod now they know their power tongues or pricks all the same now you pay for the sins of the fathers and the mothers Our lowly vision of ourselves Tod we must lose our lowly vision move out and fight the mother and father figures holding us back today none to fight androgynous kids no true identity how easy but have they never to feel jealous fists and teeth after lust in the afternoon the big cats bite and scratch gently her lips loose now she comes off fast pulling your buttocks into the sofa shake tells the girl below she is getting what is not in church Nothing new with you and Helen today home happy and content last night It was fine with the woman today relating not afraid doing a job on the magazine stimulating Tod I do love you let me fry sausages leave two for lunch-time Sean rings Met a director wants a writer religious man if a meths drinker asks for money takes him in and feeds him going on his own with family few films now for television coming to the exes of five years told him about you want to meet Sure anything not mixed with the big one hundred percent tonight is the night of the group for Helen helping each other like you when the drink was not now Tod a girl in the group suffered from her father belonged to a rigid sect beaten sadistically now terrible impulses to torture children slashes herself as a child when she hates herself needs tremendous control passing children when good she wants to snatch have a baby most of us in the group exaggerate feelings about *Are you her child*
Tod a man there has no sex he wets the bed terribly protective to them when I've held a tiny baby in my arms afterwards terrible

fantasies only got to open my arms and drop it will be smashed and dead second's loss of control Tod how I see being helpless

*Her fear of responsibility your fear of*

Awareness of harm that could of course I'm not going to drop it in fantasy I go hot all over Helen you do not desire to harm

*Will you be smashed will*

Tremendous awareness of vulnerability of child from one's own experience as one identifying with one if I love myself I can love the child if one is ambivalent about oneself is ambivalent about

*Ambivalent*

Dreaming at Helens last Christmas the huge tower again college tunnels lead out for escape lowering coffins from the chapel waiting for Helen does not come to you meeting students you stand and speak Gaelic It is time the language was used by some students leap to support an American pushes Society of Gaels undreamed help in rules of procedure stop you think of one in the college someone is dead a funeral passes flower strewn into the sending-down room with tunnel machinery you cry Sssshhhh a funeral behind you giggles a girl pushes you go down to where the wheels and wires move on the cliffside thugs jeer as you go to your new dormitory crowded unhappy you find Sean who writes before you Helen reads what you wrote Tod I do not like if Not said only thought love It takes away from an optimust commune on the scrubbed benches rare simplicity Are you angry because of you Helen No no but bad writing too on the group feelings holding a child ambivalent But that is straight talk Tod it does not real well I must criticise If you want Helen you must help me About the adolescent Tod you jump over six years why do you not want to face the second part of Helen I want to get on with You must face it stop avoiding you past Tod face it now Now try to face Helen happy in Saturday morning sun clouds appear a cliché in the afternoon her evening face clears on Sunday she vamps you in black stockings scared of herself I must make this work for outside a person rings for Helen hides you answer for the girl in the basement Why did he ring ours darling see the flowered hats descend the scrubbed faces enter below you enter her standing up and playing her new part exciting face to face secret sinking down a temple idol squats above the prayer meeting Do they hear do they *know* Try to face it get down into what happened to you imagine Uncle Fred listens as you lie on the moor river pools hiding trout vast hinterland unexplored the White Stone Spring endlessly pushes its sweet water endlessly into the burn a cure for dying men flattened monoliths on their bier of stones mysterious how they came a thousand years a thousand people now one dying man banished by a girl brings him milk over the heather past the dark loch which claims her in thirty years despairing sheep skitter with stupid faces you leap the groined earth resilient hidden below no people the shuddering Loch hides gran Annes Water Horse half-man Washing by the loch the Water Horse rose up to her put his head in her lap the grinning teeth sharp ears he went to sleep softly she undid her apron strings crept away last year a thin body bobbed in the water horse won at last a huge hole in the matted weedmud was it a bomb Fin heard one night falling on the moor no sound after buried deep in fathomless peat penetrated was it a heap of stones Martha knew and told one stone for each soul who departed the village midwife laid them out then came to pray with a stone for the pile kicked apart by pagan boys after football now no water horse no cairn for you nothing but the elder's curse unhappy youth trudge the barrens the banal message from the oracle eats into her mystery female mirth anguish You will kill your father and draw your androgynous sword Oedipus Resink your flesh in her you lift the hinge of the beaten copper mask Working in the afternoons now working mornings earning afternoons for the lump you put figures in books soothe screams of pain from small people who took on could not cope the grinding jaws of free enterprise tighten around their premium product madam has a premium price pay up missus or else I've got problems your boss speaks to you outside I was an engineer before the change of life painting learning exhibiting the mayor gives a glass of cooking sherry the six intellectuals stand nodding wisely at some rubbish you must know the rules before you look at Dali or Magritte they paint a finger an egg watch a man in a bowler hat you say that draughtmanship draw you into the picture then to tell you but a mess of paint no form random could be a damp patch on the ceiling if it does not hit something deep at once it does not work why should it the damp spot just as good maybe better more random than messing by boys who cannot bother to learn I trained as an engineer now I live to paint tell me your philosophy Tod you say Not british greeks dead look to Europe travelling to work a girl flutes in the white tunnel the trains do not drown the notes her bed on the floor buskers will be pros Helen I want to investigate the King's Head full of boys and girls in castoff clothes cast off music to stir the gentle folk half of bitter for one and six you know you should not play with fire drinking with her silent beside the closed face tattered theatre posters drama of being an alcoholic maybe playing a chosen role the actors come past self-concious looking for themselves do not stop Helen being angry I am going home Not angry love with a smile she stays Tod I am jealous of your drinking I watched another addict killing you are silent Mum does not approve you return to Dad

# 11

# SEAN

Tod discussed *Helen* with me many times as he was writing it. It was during the autumn after he left college and went to live with Helen in Islington. The writing is influenced by his recent exposure to Existentialism; although, as always, he was attempting to do "something different", the links with modern French literature and also Joyce will be obvious, in particular the selection of the second person present tense, which I know was suggested to him by a book of Michel Butor's. At first glance, the work appears to be arbitrarily obtuse, unnecessarily and pretentiously difficult and opaque; one's immediate reaction is to shrug and to refuse to pander to the selfish whims of one who does not seem to want to communicate with us at all. But this would be a mistake: the writing, once one has got the general sense, is fairly easy to follow and is quite consistent in style. It was, he told me, the most difficult task he had undertaken and it must have created great strain in the relationship with Helen: it will be obvious that he was using his day to day life with her quite ruthlessly, in order to provide a framework within which to explore himself. Few women would have tolerated this; Helen not only tolerated it, she encouraged him enormously; coming home each night from the editing of fiction, she would sit down and read and criticise what Tod had managed to squeeze out during the day.

He was determined to write a full-length novel in this style and he held to his task for more than three months, but was quite unable to carry on with it after he moved out to Notting Hill, partly because he no longer had the solid base of his life with Helen within which to work.

As we should anticipate, Tod starts right at the beginning, describing the first "bare sheet" almost as he inserts it into the typewriter, whilst sitting in the tiny study in the newly-converted flat. Tod's working corner was situated in what had been the lavatory, a circumstance which intrigued and pleased him at the time.

So once again, despite the experimental nature of the writing, we see Tod compelled to adhere slavishly to chronology to provide him with the outward frame of the work, as though his sense of passing time was the only one he could trust to hold events together. This results at one level in the production of a sort of semi-fictional diary of the day to day relationship of Helen and Tod (From what I know of them, I can state categorically that the facts far outweigh the fiction; in any case, Tod had no strong awareness of any strict dividing line between fact and fiction and would have argued that no such arbitrary line could be drawn). At another level, we see Tod dealing with his memories, thoughts and dreams; using the second person present tense, he attempts to bring all this material together on the page as it "happens" inside his head.

He told me at this time that his search was for a style of writing that could "show present, past and possible future within the same paragraph." (Hence his great admiration for Simenon, who Tod maintained does just that, without putting the slightest strain on his reader.) Tod's decision to eliminate all punctuation, apart from capital letters to indicate direct speech was an old-fashioned attempt to simulate the flow of a mind, an attempt which is to my mind self-defeating; are our thoughts really devoid of full stops and commas?

It is one thing to try to simulate a mind in motion using only words; to succeed in sustaining it is something else. Tod told me he hoped to let the words run on "indefinitely" without using the device of paragraphing at all, as it broke up the flow. He did not succeed; *Helen* is a series of broken paragraphs, because the material presenting from his mind was overwhelming; because selection is inevitable and one has to stem the flow long enough to take some of it down. He did experiment for a short time with a tape-recorder and includes a taped dialogue, worked up later, between himself and Helen.

Tod had an earlier plan for his book and he adhered to it for six weeks or so; this was to alternate the stream of consciousness paragraphs with pieces of quite traditional narrative, his notion being to link these together, each time he broke from one mode to the other by means of an association of ideas.

Indeed, he showed me some thirty or forty pages of writing of this kind; it had an unsettling effect when read, being neither fish nor fowl, as I put it to him, but some undesirable and unconvincing hybrid. However, the connections are there now, between *Helen* and the *Boy* and *Fin* pieces: I can find correspondence and associations in many places still. Was this an attempt to symbolise his difficulty in reconciling the inner and outer aspects of his life? Or is it that Tod had to keep returning obsessively to the same few themes from his childhood? Personally, my view encompasses both the above notions; and we must never forget either that a long-term creative work, like Topsy, just grows.

As for the business of Tod's alcoholism, which he discusses more than once in *Helen*, although not in any depth: my own reading on this unfashionable subject had made me suspect Tod was one of those men who are, in the Freudian sense, arrested at the *genital* stage of their development. Such men are unable to make any permanent relationship with a woman; although excessively interested in the whole business of human sexuality, their personal relationships tend to be short-lived and transitory. My familiarity with Tod's life and my recent close study of his writings has served to convince me that his particular pattern was indeed a *genital* one, rather than the more common *oral* one to be found in so many alcoholics. (In passing, it should be mentioned that Tod was excited to discover, from the work of Upton Sinclair and others, that so many modern writers were alcoholic. It was another scrap of encouragement to him to go on writing). The fact that Tod came from an environment which produces twelve times as many alcoholics per 100,000 as the south east of England has got its own significances, but this may not be the place to speculate upon the reasons for the high incidence of the illness of Gaeldom, apart from making the obvious assertion that

Tod's chances of becoming alcoholic were correspondingly increased. Tod may have been encouraged to write by his belief that many writers had alcoholic tendencies; it does not seem to have occured to him that he might just as easily have been an alcoholic and yet be quite illiterate.

There is a tendency in *Helen* to go in for a type of punning; a weak imitation of some earlier writers in this *genre*. Tod was very fond of puns and when stimulated by conversation would often produce one; occasionally it was good pun; more often it was Tod himself who laughed, especially if he thought he had made what he called a "trun" or a "quadrun"; puns with more than one reverberation. I must say this tendency of his, on those occasions when he was feeling exuberant for some unaccountable reason, was a sore trial to some of his friends. Many of these plays on words were scatological and sometimes his hearers were shocked; further proof, to my mind of his particular kind of immaturity. "Straight" comedy was anathema to him, so much so that many acquaintances were convinced of his humourlessness; this is far from being the truth; Tod's sense of fun was specialised and personal, however.

As I have indicated, Tod was writing at this time what he came to call "autofaction"; so far as I was able to understand the term, by "autofaction" he meant autobiographical fact (part diary, part memory), given a fictional gloss "Where he felt it required it." With Tod, there were no rules about where this gloss was to be applied; it simply happened as he went along and it usually depended on his only partly-conscious need for order and symbolism; that is what my reading gives me to understand of his methods. I am aware this will be found unsatisfactory, but in mitigation, I have to stress that Tod's working methods, such as they were (apart from pure intuition), were constantly changing; so much so that one cannot point to a piece of his writing and say instantly: "that's vintage Calum Tod." There *is* no vintage Calum Tod. One of his main problems as a writer was this failure to create an individual style and then work to perfect it. Discovering himself in a constant state of flux he was inclined to reproduce his own flux in the work of the moment.

Dreams and their undoubted significance intrigued Tod at the time of writing *Helen*. I know he was one of those persons who scarcely ever remember dreams, apart from the occasional nightmare (which has the effect of jerking the sleeper awake and thus fixing the dream in the consciousness.) The fact that Tod began to note his dreams at this time naturally resulted in his subconscious obligingly supplying them; in addition, Helen provided him with some of her own dreams, at his request. These dreams Tod wove at once into the narrative of *Helen*; one of them is recorded simply as raw notes, made on waking; the other we find used twice, first in note form and then again as part of the diary.

Comparison of these two versions of Tod's "funeral" dream does not reveal any attempt on his part at later interpretation; he probably accepted it as a simple rebirth theme, connected with his time at college, and did not wish to probe it further. There is a clue to this rebirth theme in the notes entitled Afternoon Dream; it is clear that Tod had previously dreamt of the "elaborate tunnel system for escape and for lowering down to the earth the coffins of the dead from the Abbey chapel where the monk's skull is kept in the wall in a cardboard box." (One wonders now why it never occurred to Tod to link this dream which starts with a skull to the one Helen had of him dressed up as an Elizabethan Hamlet.)

As I have said, Tod experimented with a tape-recorder during his time at Helen's flat but the only evidence of this in *Helen* is the recorded conversation they had about his motives and methods of writing at the time. He was genuinely, I know, attempting to involve Helen fully in what he was trying to do; to be fair to Tod, he said more than once that his writing at that time depended upon her entirely. (This was even truer than he realised; after all, not only was she providing him with a bed; with free and expert literary criticism; with a complete and safe environment within which he could write; she was also supplying him with much of his actual material. The selfish and ruthless use he made of their daily life together sometimes took my breath away.)

Although I should like to be more than fair to my friend, I must admit that many readings of the Helen/Tod recorded conversation leave me thinking he was not being absolutely honest with her. (I have seen the actual transcript and I can vouch for the fact that no editing or fictionalising has taken place here, apart from considerable tightening-up and the insertion of the thoughts of Tod; thoughts which are a genuine attempt to convey what he felt in the actual moment). I do not mean to suggest that Tod was being deliberately dishonest, but there is no doubt he failed to convey to Helen all of his true feelings; about the "novel" yes, perhaps, but about their relationship, no. Close attention to the way he steers the talk will make this clear. At every moment, Tod is terribly aware of the danger of committing himself, irrevocably, to Helen or to anyone else; this results in a strained and stilted conversation, from his side; in a discussion that does not, for much of the time, engage him at any deep level. He is actually watching himself, from afar; the writer busily observing his own characters as they discuss the "fiction" they are meant to create. It is a weird experience, for one who knew them so well, to watch them thus engaged in this game, the pair of them being manipulated by Tod, who, to be fair to him, is not really aware of what he is doing.

Tod later became conscious of this distortion produced in the relationship by his obsession with his need to write and it may have played a part in the mutual decision, taken later that year, that he and Helen should part.

But Helen was a stronger character than Tod in some ways; although, womanlike, she was probably more fond of Tod than he was of her, it was Helen who quietly confirmed the decision for both of them. Before Tod quite realised what was happening, he was back again with me in the bedsitter house in Notting Hill. "We parted friends," was all he was prepared to say at first, "she belongs here and I belong *there*." He meant Lewis, of course. He was very proud of his complete acceptance by Helen; in this I suspect something in Tod that has always been common in the highlander: his deep need to prove himself in the "best" places. Men have taken the high road to London from the Highlands and Islands for hundreds of years; those who succeeded in the south have sometimes later returned; as they pass Edinburgh on the way home, they raise a mocking finger in its direction. . . It is a kind of revenge for the betrayal of the Gael by the Scottish Lowlander. And it is also, of course, another example of the Gael's pride; a pride that is not untainted with snobbishness.

Something needs to be said about the ever-recurring theme of the sexual relationship of Helen and Tod. His repeated use of their physical encounters could be described as obsessive, were it not for the knowledge we have of his working methods; I refer to his great need to find a framework within which to set down his daily experience at the time. And what more powerful landmarks could there be than their repeated acts of love-making? But although Tod discovered the delights of pure sex only after he stopped drinking and purified his brain and body of the poisons of alcohol, his time with the sensual Beatrice should by now have solved his immature obsession with physicality?

This, I must admit, was my own view of the matter; although the affair with Beatrice was quite stormy at times, Tod had often assured me (in order to make me jealous?) of the extraordinary physical freedom he had found with her.

When I came to read *Helen*, however, I discovered the sexual obsession afresh; indeed, in the writings of Tod one finds far more reference to sex with Helen than one does to his relations with Beatrice. This puzzled me for a long time but I think I have now some part of the answer and it is this: although there was a new freedom with the experienced and Europeanised Beatrice and although the physical release was great (for a time, I feared Tod was going to let himself sink without thought into a life of pure sensuality) yet this was not enough in the end. Tod demanded more than simple animal release from his partners; he needed intellectual stimulation even in matters of sex and this Beatrice was not able to give him. My observation of her convinced me she was actually afraid of Tod's pretensions to writing and of the obsession she sensed in him; intuitive as she was, Beatrice became aware at some level that Tod was simply using her for his own complicated purposes; in the way he used me, and Helen, and everyone close to him at one time or another. There is a clue also to be found in the great differences between Beatrice and Helen; where Beatrice was dark, Helen was fair; where Beatrice was sensual, Helen was sophisticated; where Beatrice was intuitive, Helen was intellectual, where Beatrice was older, Helen was younger.

In truth, both women had much to give Tod; ideally, what he

demanded was someone who was a blending of the two women who had given him so much; a manifest impossibility. A pointer to this need of Tod's for a reconciliation of what he once called the "darkness with the light" is to be found in the last scene of his play *The Elder's Woman*, which now looks like an attempt to reconcile the elements of *anima* and *animus*: the fusing of the best in both male and female. (This play was actually written in Helen's flat, as their relationship was coming to an end).

As further evidence for my conclusion regarding Tod's unconscious reaching for some kind of reconciliation between what he saw as the dark feminine and the light masculine elements, I would point to the odd "scene" in *Helen* where Tod discusses the differing sexual potentialities of blondes and brunettes. (This piece was obviously inspired by a visit we paid to a current London production of *The Bacchae*, possibly the first such to use nude females). The theory, so far as I am able to follow it, suggests that brunettes are more sensual than blondes only on the surface; the truth is, according to Tod, that fair women are the true sensualists but their feelings are so deeply buried, they seldom succeed in reaching their full potential in the act of sex, because the feelings of blondes are so powerful they are afraid to give in to them, in case they "destroy" them. Obviously, the whole argument stands or falls upon whether or not one accepts that dark-skinned women are more sensual than fair-skinned women in the first place. And that is merely a generalised opinion. All it really tells us is that for Tod, sensuality equals darkness and intellect equals light. And there is nothing original in that.

It certainly does not prove anything whatsoever about the "sexual potential" of women in general, be they fair or dark. But it points to something much more interesting, that is nothing to do with sex: the deep conflict in Tod himself as he tried to decide whether he was a *dark* Celt or a *fair* Nord; both races were inextricably mixed in his Hebridean heritage. Tod always saw the Celt as creative, feminine, and the Nord as destructive, masculine. "Calvanism suits the Nord in us; it destroys the Celt," he said to me once.

In truth, both Helen and Tod had still many problems of identity and sexuality to work through. The partners in the Islington flat had, however, something powerfully in common: both Helen and Tod were engaged in an aware and single-minded quest for maturity; he through his writing, she through ruthless and often painful self-analysis. Helen was not content to let the truth about her deep needs and feelings simply percolate through to her consciousness as Tod was; she probed and thought and discussed with a self-awareness and honesty Tod was not capable of. Although he discussed their mutual problems with her, Tod was seldom fully engaged; as we have seen with the taped discussion he preferred to let his intuition do the work for him and he was quite incapable of the emotional commitment full self-revelation would have entailed. Tod never accepted that he might have something of an Oedipus complex, insisting his problems sprang from the conflict with the powerful father figures in his life; my own feeling is that the reliance he was beginning to place upon Helen convinced her of his buried oedipal feelings towards her and precipitated her decision they should part, months before they need have, according to Tod's selfish reading of the situation. Helen knew far more about psychology than Tod and also had a better grasp altogether of the complexities of personal relationships. (I knew kind-hearted Martha, his mother, well; as the eldest, there is no doubt Tod received an enormous amount of maternal love and security in the first three years of his life). Helen's growing suspicion, which she did not always hide, convinced me, at least, of the developing danger; the danger of his becoming dependent upon the safe "maternal" environment Helen was providing at the time. Insistence upon personal independence and lone integrity was even stronger, albeit quieter, within Helen than it was in Tod himself; Tod may well have sunk, for a few months at least, into a passive accepting role; Helen knew she would be unable to provide the right atmosphere for any length of time. So, although Tod imagined the decision to part was his, in reality it was Helen's.

# 12

# CALUM

He decided to go to the little Italian cafe by the cinema. There would be an hour left in which to buy all he needed at the supermarket on the corner of Kensington Church Street, which stayed open until eight o'clock on Friday nights.

The waitress was dark, with an intense look. She ignored him and took the orders of two couples who had come in after him. She spoke harshly into the speaking tube leading down to the kitchen:

"Doubleegg cheeps twice!"

She came over at last and he ordered an omelette and a green salad. It was the best meal to buy there, he remembered.

That afternoon, in the office where he worked for four hours a day, Miss Fawcett had come to sit by him. She was wearing a loose brown dress, tightly drawn in at the waist by a green scarf. She sat with her legs apart and the dress fell between her thighs. She had scratched at her leg once through the dress and he heard the tiny rustle of the material rubbing against her stocking.

He did not know why, but he was sure that Miss Fawcett wore stockings and not tights, like the other women. They had discussed the amounts due to the customers who had returned faulty parts to the store downstairs. As she rose to go, he had said:

"I'd like to work here until the spring, Jacqueline."

"You can stay as long as you like."

He needed the money, and as Miss Fawcett did not concern herself with the matter of his income tax and insurance payments, he could keep all his earnings. In this way, he could live on what he could earn in twenty hours each week.

That morning, he had said goodbye to Helen in her flat in North London, where he had lived for four months after his return from college.

"It has been a wonderful eighteen months. We have both developed as people."

It was true, certainly for him. Close contact with a girl, younger than he, who had been to Oxford, who was part of the sophisticated south, had changed him. But in what ways? She, at least, had no doubts:

"Darling Calum, you have helped me enormously."

A young man with a beard sat down opposite him and ordered a plate of spaghetti and a glass of water. Calum glanced at him and then he unfolded his copy of *The Evening Standard*:

ENERGY CRISIS GROWS

His food came and he began to eat. The omelette was not over-cooked and the salad was ample and fresh. Just as before!

He had lived in Notting Hill twice previously, the last time only eighteen months ago. He liked the area; the ever-open shops; the vitality of the multi-racial young people who inhabited the thousands of bed-sitters in the still-elegant Victorian streets. He was living in the same house as the last time, in the room above the one he'd occupied when. . .

"This is a poor portion of spaghetti!"

The young man opposite was complaining to the waitress in a cultured voice. She stared at him without comprehending, shrugged, and went away. The man took a sip of his water and, still grumbling, began to eat his meal.

Calum noticed a woman of about thirty-five who was watching him from a nearby table. Her shapely legs were crossed; they were tightly encased in light grey tights; her saffron skin showed through them.

An Italian, perhaps, by her dark, elegant clothes. He began to read the paper again but the thought was now in the back of his mind: Helen and I are free.

The waitress brought his coffee and forgot to add it to the bill. He drank it and prepared to go. Whilst shrugging into the wool-lined coat that Helen had bought for him the previous winter, he noticed that the woman was also getting ready to leave.

Was she hoping that he would speak to her?

"There's a coffee to go on," he told the proprietor as he handed him the bill.

The man began to fill a plastic cup with coffee.

"Coffee to go, sir."

He pushed the cup across the counter.

"To go on the bill!"

The man laughed at his mistake. Language problems, we all have them. The woman was by Calum's shoulder now and he glanced at her. The incident of the coffee had given her courage and she smiled at him with a sort of warm complicity. Although she did not move, he fancied that he could feel the soft pressure from her shoulder.

He picked up his change quickly and wet out into the cold, pulling up the collar of his coat, which he knew restricted his vision. He did not look back, feeling a surge of desire for this woman who had offered herself to him.

Or had she done so?

The story of his life; missed opportunities. He strode rapidly away towards the corner of the street. Approaching the supermarket, he turned to look back. She had not followed.

He picked up a wire basket and looked about him. There was a long queue at each of the checkouts, mainly of tired women doing their weekend shopping after work.

Voices were suddenly raised. A drab, middle-aged woman was shouting at a girl wearing a sheep-skin coat:

"Bleedin' furriner!"

The girl turned to her and spoke quietly:

"Please, control yourself!"

She had the kind of sliding American accent that grated in his ears.

"We don't want you in our country. In 1940, we stood alone!"

The woman was near hysteria. What deep rooted problem was she trying to grapple with? Had a U.S. serviceman, during the war...

"You're finished, you British! Do you hear?"

The girl was angry now. People turned away, embarrassed.

He went to find the television monitor that protected the store from shop-lifters. It still hung high in an aisle, near the bacon display.

In the past, he had surreptitiously watched himself on the grey screen, moving to and from the camera, trying for a close-up view.

Hadn't a work of art last year at the Hayward Gallery consisted of just that—two television cameras and a screen to watch yourself on?

In the same exhibition, a whole room had been given over to a large circle of rounded stones laid out on the floor; stones exactly like those that lay in thousands on the beach near his home in Lewis.

What did it mean?

He made a mental note to visit the current exhibition that weekend. Watercolours and drawings by Cezanne, the man who had painted that ugly group of shapeless nude women bathers which he had watched people stare at with awe in the National gallery.

Perhaps he would discover what Cezanne had been trying to do?

He was not able to line himself up correctly, so as to appear on the monitor screen. *They've moved the camera.*

He had to think of everthing; soap, salt, toothpaste, honey, milk and crispbread, eggs, bacon, fruit—the food he needed to keep him over the weekend. It was too expensive to eat out all the time.

Nostalgically, he thought now of Helen standing over the stove, a cigarette protruding at an inimitable angle from her lips, preparing his favourite meal of liver and bacon. She worked on a magazine, in the fiction department, and she had bought their supper each day from a shop in Drury Lane.

She was several years his junior, but he always said they were about the same age, emotionally at least. What had he meant? In any case, it was true that they were both attempting to come to terms with deep-seated problems; problems that had made Helen injure herself; how shocked the matronly ladies had been, in the posh loo at Kings X!—that had caused him to descend into the gutter before his rehabilitation began.

A few nights ago in her flat, on the double divan, he had lain beneath her, completely passive. She had taken over the direction of their joining, feeling towards the fullness of her femininity. At the end, he had groaned aloud, the sounds torn from him by the waves of sensation she had aroused in his body.

Was all that finished?

Before they fell asleep last night, she had said:

"I do believe it was meant that we should meet."

Had she mentioned God? They had been to church once, at Easter. They sat in one of the side pews in St. Martin's off Trafalgar Square, holding hands and gazing at the banks of daffodils.

She said nothing. Afterwards, he told her:

"It's the only church I care for. They feed down and outs in the basement."

He went down there, once, but he had been too embarrassed to speak to anybody, least of all to the fervid women who were ladling out the soup. The ragged resentful men had frightened him and he returned thankfully to the cosy A.A. meeting in the room above.

He climbed the four flights of stairs to his room. It measured fourteen feet by twelve and it was crowded with a small bed, two kitchen chairs, two rickety tables, a small chest of drawers, an old wardrobe and a rocking chair. In one corner there was a wash basin and a gas ring stood beside it on top of a small cupboard.

On each end of the mantel, above the gas fire, there stood a huge black bottle. One of them had a stump of yellow candle stuck in the neck. Were these some of the props used in the rituals when...

The previous year, when he had lived in the room beneath, he lay in bed listening to the strange noises from above his head. They had come from the room he now occupied.

Later, he met the girl who then lived in Number 21. She was wearing a long black cloak that trailed on the ground. Her white face was framed by long dark hair, parted in the middle.

"I'm a witch."

He was fascinated and a little scared. So that explained the sound of horns and chanting in the night!

She promised to try magic to help him publish his short story. It had not worked, if indeed she remembered to try it. Had she?

They were white witches, he reminded himself now, fingering one of the bottles gingerly. His story was about a sophisticated and beautiful woman, married to a diplomat. She had left the Hebrides many years before, but she still possessed second sight.

The Gift.

He changed his socks and put on an old pair of slippers; a Christmas present from his mother, two years ago. Or was it three?

After stripping off his shirt he washed his face in the lukewarm water that dribbled from the tap on the basin; the basin where he had to wash his dirty dishes as well. And if the nights got really cold. . .

He looked at himself closely in the mirror; he pulled in his stomach and pushed out his chest, turning a little in order to see the muscles of his back and shoulders. Although he could not see them, he knew that his legs were thick and that his buttocks protruded behind him.

"Made for swinging a kilt!"

Helen had admired his body:

"You'd make a splendid model, darling."

She was the same height as he was, five feet eight inches, in her shoes.

He examined his face again. A deep furrow cut right across the forehead, half-way between the eyes and the hair-line. Had it got less prominent since his meeting with Helen? His nose stuck out.

"Alice calls it your bird-look."

When you thought about it, wasn't there a questioning look about his face? Like some large bird, with its head up and slightly to one side.

Abruptly, he turned away and pulled on a purple sweater. Another gift from Helen.

It was a good feeling, that Sunday, sitting quietly outside the exhibition hall, alone, with the thick catalogue on his knee, smoking a cigarette. There was no need to discuss the pictures with anyone.

*He paints by means of patches of overlapping colour.*

Should he send the catalogue to Margery, who was now teaching art in the Highlands and would not be able to see the exhibition?

Or was he just looking for an excuse to contact her again?

He had met Margery when she came to the Hebrides to finish a project for her diploma. That same summer, in London, she had come to his room in the house in Westbourne Street. In the autumn she had returned to Scotland to teach.

Why should he want to resume contact with Margery? She was years his junior. He visualised her slim body and the firm adolescent breasts. The nipples had been pink. Were they still?

It had been his flirtation with art?

He decided that he would not send her the catalogue.

He had to think things out, once and for all. The winter loomed ahead of him and there would be plenty of time for thought.

Had he not so arranged it?

On Monday morning, the housekeeper toiled to the top floor to collect his rent and stayed to talk.

"Have you decided what you're going to do yet?"

"I'm not going back to journalism."

It was as far as he had got. In the past few years, he had worked for a number of dull magazines during his times in London.

"You waste your energies..."

Was it true that he was wasting his life away, misdirecting his efforts, chopping and changing? Last year, he had gone to the college for mature students and he had been accepted for a university at the end of his course. Now he had turned that chance down.

Where was he going?

Since stopping drinking so many years ago, as it seemed now, he had never settled or made any kind of permanent life for himself. Instead, he would say:

"Two years in London, alternated with two years in Lewis. That's the life for me!"

Brave words and his listeners had been envious. But they sounded a bit hollow now. He had lived in another bed-sitter ten years ago; his life was outwardly the same now as it had been then.

He had been convinced, only four months ago, that he and Helen would be able to work out what they each wanted from life, if they lived together. He had never lived with a woman, as man and wife, before.

It had not happened. Instead, he had begun to feel trapped, although she insisted on extracting no promises from him.

Had she been feeling the same? In any case, she had been quite in agreement with him when he told her that he had taken a room.

They had parted as good friends on Friday morning. Would they really be happier, living as single, separate individuals?

During his vacation from the college, he had discussed with her those writings of the existentialists which had excited him and he had thought at the time that her reactions had been favourable.

Freedom of choice as an individual. Was this what you lost when you agreed to live with someone? *Freedom to choose who you were.*

Did he want to return, permanently, to the islands, to live quietly on the croft with his mother? Was that what he had *chosen?*

He did not know.

Dimly, he felt that his unease had nothing much to do with whom he lived or where. For the time being, in any case, he wanted to be alone, in order to think about his life.

He had accomplished nothing.

Why?

That was what he had to discover.

Down in the basement of the offices where he worked was kept the stationery; cabinets and files and paper of all kinds. A retired printer, a large quiet man who smoked a pipe and whose name was Ted, was in charge. Calum had gone there to ask for a box-file and cards for a new filing system that he had planned with Miss Fawcett.

Ted took him around the metal shelves and showed him what he had in stock.

"There's a ten week delivery date on some of these."

Would he still be working for Automatic Spares in ten weeks time?

"Have you anything else"

Ted showed him a parcel of rectangular cards with rounded corners.

"These are obsolete since they got the new computer."

Calum handled the springy cards with pleasure. They were just the right size, feel and shape. They had no lines on them; they were beautifully blank. He had a sudden urge to write on the bland and creamy surfaces.

"Have you a box to put them in?"

A plan began to shape itself in his mind.

"Two boxes?"

Ted reached up on a shelf and brought down two dusty box files. He blew on them and pulled out the little drawers.

"These will take the cards. But why do you need two?"

"I have a new idea."

Already in his mind he was calling it the Plan. He was not sure what exactly it consisted of, but he knew that the cards were necessary to it.

As he went up the concrete stairs to the offices he could see already one of the boxes and a stack of the cards in his room, on the little table in the corner by the window.

In his mind's eye, he picked up the first card. What would he write on it?

*Birth*

What next? Did he need dates, times, places?

Are places, for instance, that important to a man's life? Would he not develop—or not develop—in the same way anywhere?

It would not be an autobiography, of course, or anything of that nature. And perhaps it would not be a good idea to follow a rigid chronology—like the filing systems he was used to. He would let himself relax; it was, after all, his own system and he need not be anxious about its efficiency.

No Miss Fawcett would ever come to him to demand information, or figures, which had to be instantly available. By not using an index, he would be able to mix the cards up and change the order at any time.

If this had happened before that, then. . .

On the way home that evening he stopped at a stationers and bought three pencils; the type with soft lead in them.

"And could I have a large eraser, please?"

The box with the cards was tucked under his arm. He did not want to waste time in preparing a meal so he went to the Bakeaway near the underground station and bought a baked potato with minced meat.

When he had eaten it and brewed the strong tea that he liked in the earthenware mug that Helen had given him, he made his preparations.

He took the shade off the bedside lamp and transferred the lamp to the table in the corner. He wiped the box with a damp cloth and set it up on the right hand side of the table, next to the wall. To the left of the table he arranged the cards; to the right, he laid out the pencils and the eraser. A small space remained in the middle for working on.

He was ready.

But where could he begin?

He closed his eyes and tried to summon up a scene. All he could think of was an incident that had taken place in the office that afternoon.

The head salesman was speaking angrily to him:

"That's not what I told you to do!"

Frinton was a big man of about his own age, aggressive and confident. He was the company's top seller and he bore the knowledge around with him like an aura of some kind.

"But I have paperwork to prove that..."

"To hell with your piffling paper work! If you'd done what I..."

He stopped listening and observed his antagonist. For there was no doubt about it; he and Frinton were facing each other in latter's office, exactly like creatures in the forest. Apes?

Calum's first reaction had been one of anxiety and guilt. Perhaps he had made a mistake? No doubt he was in the wrong again. He vaguely remembered failing to make a phone call and writing a memo instead. He had not felt able to question a stranger on the telephone. There were days when he...

Today was not one of those days. He had the box and the cards under the desk outside, ready to take them home.

He leaned over Frinton's desk and picked up the order. He crumpled it in his hand and tossed it towards the waste basket.

"There's no need to lose the head."

Deliberately, he had used the slang expression. Yet he felt no anger towards Frinton. Did this mean that he was not afraid of him?

Now, he visualised the true ending to the scene in Frinton's office. He stepped around the desk.

"Get up."

Frinton rose to his feet and they grappled. Calum broke away and struck with his right, deep into the expense-account fat around Frinton's midriff. But the man was tough. He came back, swinging...

Miss Fawcett stood in the doorway, wide-eyed...

In fact, Frinton's face had showed a quick, calculated change when Calum spoke so firmly. Had he been thinking:

"Beter not to antagonise the staff. . ."

He had calmed down and repeated his instructions with a forced, patient, reasonableness. Calum had gone back to his desk and as he sat down the anger had come to him at last:

"Bastard!"

Now he wrote the word out on a card in large letters. *File under B.*

He screwed the card up and threw it on the floor. After a few seconds, he got up and put it in the plastic bin by the wash basin.

As he did so, he saw the saucepan on the gas ring and he remembered his grandmother.

She was a strong woman with broad hips and powerful legs.

No wonder!

He had seen her carry a creel at seventy-five and skim the turf off a peatbank at eighty. She refused to take fuel from the family and insisted on cutting her own peats; although his mother had come back from Canada to look after her in her old age, Ann had never liked his father although he had been born only across the bay.

Now he was getting somewhere. He picked up the first card on the pile and inscribed carefully on it:

GRANDMOTHER

Born? Old Ann had died when eighty-five years old.

Born on the Isle of North Rona.

She had black eyes, which are rare in the islands. Wasn't there a story about the survivors from the Spanish Armada?

"The dark-eyed girls are very passionate."

Had a Spaniard crawled ashore on North Rona? The island had been evacuated at about the time of Ann's birth. Or long before it? He preferred to think it was later.

What was it like to be old and alone? Having borne nine children, to be left by yourself in a room, to brood on the need to accept help from others at last?

What had Ann thought, when the five dollar bills came to her at Christmas?

Conscience money; how would old Ann express that to herself in Gaelic?

He remembered his mother saying:

"She gives me a hard time..."

Yet, it had been Martha, the seventh daughter, that Ann had chosen to give the croft to. In return for...

Would Fin and Martha have stayed had it not been for the Depression? Would they not have returned to Canada had the situation improved?

Would he not have been brought up as a Canadian?

He got up and prowled about the room. Catching sight of himself in the mirror behind the open door of the wardrobe, he made a face; he raised his eyebrows until the furrow in his forehead was deeply etched.

Was that how he would look when he was old?

He put on the heavy coat and went out for a walk.

The grey street was cold under the lights and a smell of putrefaction came up from some of the basements. The coal cellars of the Victorians are stacked with plastic bags full of unnameable rubbish.

Outside the underground station he was approached by a thin young man, shivering in light clothes, holding a bundle of newspapers.

"Workers Press, buy the Workers Press, get the Tories out."

He had said it a thousand times; Calum could hear it in the lack of conviction in the voice.

Why did he go on trying to sell the papers?

"Fourpence, man."

Calum tucked the paper into his pocket. May as well find out what the Trots are saying this week; it provides a balance.

As he moved away, a policeman who was proceeding along Notting Hill hurried his step a little and approached the paper seller. Calum paused, half-turned to hear the conversation.

He was just too far away.

The policeman turned his head and saw him. He was very young, younger even than the paper seller, with the pale skin of a red-head. He stared suspiciously at Calum.

Calum moved away slowly, with a nonchalant air, and walked into a nearby food store that stayed open late. He sensed the policeman following him.

*I must look suspicious to him?*

He wandered about inside, glancing at the shelves, trying to think of something he needed to buy; he could see the young copper peering at him through the windows.

Calum fought the rising tide of guilt as he stared at the stack of butter, cheese and bacon in the cold display.

*Bastard!*

He bought a slab of cheese and paid for it under the eyes of the ' policeman.

He walked outside, turned left, strolled along Notting Hill Gate.

*Will he follow me?*

A feeling of panic did not quite overwhelm him.

At the street corner, he walked very wide. He could not see the policeman.

Before he put the key in the lock, he had another cautious look.

*Musn't let him think I know he's watching me.*

There was no sign now of the young man under the helmet that was too big for his boyish face.

He washed himself all over, standing on the newspaper, brushed his teeth, and went to bed.

Someone was banging on the door of number 21. It was nearly midnight and he was falling asleep.

"Telephone!"

It was Helen. She sounded very subdued and there were long pauses in their conversation which he tried to fill. Finally, there was just a quietly crackling silence between them; as though each of them was separately connected to outer space.

She tried too hard, she observed herself too much, waiting for the effects promised her by the Freudians.

"I am not *feeling* this separation."

"Please, trust your intuition, your instinct!"

"Yes. . .shall we meet?"

"Later. . ."

For the first few nights he had not slept well, rising every two hours from his thoughts to turn the light on, the fire, make a cup of tea, smoke a cigarette.

Yet, there was a part of him that was enjoying the solitude.

That morning he had received a letter from his mother.

"Reading between the lines of your letter I can see that you and Helen..."

The snow and ice had gone and in place of it had come the rain. At least, it was milder.

"I do not blame her, if she could not settle here; how often have I regretted..."

"But I know now, that it is the best place in the country for old people..."

The best place in the country for *old* people!

How old did he feel?

He had thought that a new life had begun for him when he stopped drinking. To live most of the time without guilt or remorse, to wake up in a dry bed and know how he had got there, to walk along the street without fear...

That had been enough, until...

He sat by the gas fire, looking at the white narrow bed in the corner of the room. He got up and went to the table, selected a blank card and wrote:

CALUM

Calum stood by the rough stone walls of the cottage reading the bible by the light of the setting sun. He read slowly, in English. Whenever he had a good mouthful ready he translated the words aloud into Gaelic. Calum could read English but not Gaelic, but he understood Gaelic better.

Ann, of the brown hair and black eyes, stood beside him and waited for the psalm. Her voice was pure and she could hold the chant longer than he could. She was entirely illiterate; the clash of the two cultures had left its mark on the island already, at the turn of the twentieth century.

The ululations rose over the oat-straw thatch and blew away on the breeze that came across the island from the west, from the direction of *Tir na n-Og*.

Much later, the boy named this fabled place the Isle of Nog.

Calum was a fisherman in his young days before he suffered the wound in his leg that would never close. He owned a Zulu, a half-decked full-bellied boat from the east coast with a mast that rose seventy feet into the sky, thick at the base and tapering to the top far above.

Below, in the fish hold, Calum and Ann lay together on the pungent dyed nets before he sailed for the summer fishing in the year of their marriage.

"Bring the fire, woman," Calum had said.

The fishing was good that year.

They had nine children in all and the boy's mother was the seventh daughter. Martha had the gift of healing the King's Sickness by touch and water. But, so far as was known, she did not have the gift of the sight.

The man from the Parish came from the town in a gig pulled by a grey mare the day after the funeral.

He went into cottage Number 13 as Ann watched from next door.

The two children rushed out almost at once and ran to her. The man with the black hat followed them, exasperated, and spoke to her:

"There is a place for orphans in the town."

Ann looked down at the sobbing children who clung to her skirt. She looked at the man, and at his mare cropping the grass from the top of the thick cottage walls.

"You mean, the Poorhouse?"

Her English was hesitant.

"It is a good place. We have several children there already."

"Can you not see they do not want to go with you?"

The man looked at the children and then at her. He was not very interested. Ann spoke quickly:

"Leave them with me."

The man was astonished.

"How will you feed them?"

Ann looked down at the little girl who was peeping up at her with suspended breath.

"They will have what we have ourselves."

The man was surprised and pleased to be rid of his duty so easily. He patted Ann on the shoulder and felt the firm flesh.

"You are a lady! A real lady, madam."

He turned, jerked the mare's head away from the succulent grass, led her back to the road and swung into the driving seat.

The gig clattered off. The man did not look back.

Ann had saved the two orphans. Later the lad died in France and the girl got consumption.

He was having trouble with two of the women who worked for him on the invoicing and filing at Automatic Spares.

One was a young African, recently married, who he thought carried her domestic worries with her to work. Aggressive and self-pitying by turns, she had angered by her attitudes a middle-aged woman who had been born and brought up in London.

Was there a hidden colour-consciousness at work? He would have to be careful not to appear...

There had been black people on the islands for forty years; all were Pakistanis. *Daoine Dubh*. They started off selling cheap clothing from suitcases to crofters' wives, bumping over the narrow roads in their little vans. In the past, they had walked, then they had bicycles.

Progress...

Now there were shops in the town with strange Arabic names above the doors.

Last summer, he had been struck by the beauty of one of the girls behind the counter of such a shop. He had gone inside, pretending that he wanted something.

"You are not from the islands?"

"My father is from the islands and my mother from Pakistan."

She had the fine bones of her mother and the eyes and colour of a Celt.

"I speak Urdu and English."

"No Gaelic?"

She laughed and shook her head.

"A great pity!"

Deirdre Mohammed...

In the mornings he tried to follow a routine. He would rise at eight o'clock, when he heard the radio in the room next door come on for the news. He would boil water in the saucepan and make tea, which he drank sitting by the gas fire in his old dressing-gown.

The dressing-gown was made of a towelling material of an ochre colour. Beatrice had made it for him, before they went to Italy for a holiday together.

How many years ago was it?

They had met on a train; to be more precise they had met on the platform at Kings Cross, when she had asked him to look after her luggage whilst she made a telephone call to her mother.

Later, he had said to her:

"They should put a brass plaque on the platform where we met!"

She was a supervisor in a large hotel in the West End; one of those expensive hotels which are usually full of Americans, Europeans, tourists and businessmen.

Beatrice had been married, once, and she was a few years older than he.

Before Beatrice he had lived alone; his monk period he had called it.

She was sensual and used to having a man in her life. She had a beautiful torso like a Greek carving, with large breasts that rose under his touch, the nipples erecting under her satisfied gaze.

He had been eager to learn from her but she had said:

"There is plenty of time...later, we'll do all kinds of exciting things..."

Now, he wondered if he had been afraid of her? Afraid of her delight in...

In the flesh?

Should he make out a card for Beatrice? Perhaps he could simply include her on a general card under the heading...

*Sex*

That would not be fair; if anyone deserved a card to herself it was Beatrice.

Had she not been the one who had...? Perhaps not. No.

Today, he must buy some coloured pencils, in order to give different emphases to different subjects.

In Italy they had stayed in Sorrento, where he had had his little accident.

Did the Hotel staff believe that the blood on the sheets and the pillows had come from his nose?

It had not been a happy holiday and on the last day, on Capri, both of them angry at the milling crowds and with each other, she had decided to leave him on the spot.

At the last minute, she changed her mind and they recovered their good humour in the garden of the Villa San Michele. Nobody could nurse a grievance there for very long.

On the croft in the Hebrides, on a midsummer midnight, in the twilight, he had mounted her among the irises and she groaned and pulled at the stubborn leaves.

Instinctively, she had turned her back to him.

He had been scared of being seen, anxiously casting his eyes at the cliffs when he should have been...

At that time, his inhibitions had been stronger in the Hebrides than they were when he was in London. At *that* time?

On the bus going to work that afternoon he noted a slogan painted on a wall in Ladbroke Grove in large red letters:

CANCER IS A DISEASE CAUSED BY UNHAPPY WORK

On the wall approaching the underground station a few weeks before he had seen, painted in black letters a foot high:

ONE IN TEN GO MAD     ONE IN FIVE BREAKS DOWN,

He sometimes got the feeling that life in London was within a hair's breadth of breaking down.

The inefficiency, the carelessness, the bad service, the heaps of rubbish in the street, the unhappy faces of the passers by.

Was he trying to convince himself that he would be happier in Lewis after all?

*Life is real, there.*

What did he mean?

The school in the village had been one of the few places with a lavatory when he was a child. He remembered the first time he had gone to use it.

He had stared down at the child-size pedestal; it was totally different to the concrete trench in the byre at home. It had not occurred to him that he was supposed to sit on the wet porcelain. He had learned to squat and he took down his shorts and squatted carefully over the tiny bowl.

He smiled now, as he thought of the anxious little boy, who always had to do things the hard way; because he was too proud to ask?

His aim had been poor, the target unsighted and the ammunition soft. He tried not to feel sorry for the child but he found it hard now not to give way to a little self-pity.

He would have to be careful of self-pity.

Later that day, the headmaster had marched him outside, into the yard where the toilets were. Grant had humiliated him by opening the privy door and pointing angrily at the brown stains.

From then on had he not feared the headmaster?

For years now, running water had been installed in all the crofts. And the septic tanks were poisoning the ground.

His work at Automatic Spares was interfering with his plan. New systems had been introduced for the sales and extra duties had resulted for his little department. In spite of his determination to keep his mind free for thinking about his life, Calum found himself unable to do so for very long.

He spent many hours in his room, each morning and evening and weekend, alone, not talking to anyone.

When he was able to forget the anxieties of his job, he could not bring his mind to concentrate on his past in any organised way.

The mind flits about, was how he put it to himself. He would go out into the dank streets and walk for an hour and then go to bed.

Day succeeded day in this way, and the box file remained empty. Through his hands he would shuffle the two or three cards he had marked, and subjects for many others would spring to his mind:

*The Key*

*Alcohol*

But he was afraid to make out cards for these and others until he was ready to deal with them.

Think them through...

Perhaps he needed a system, after all?

"Begin at the beginning," Fin would say, and go on to quote the Gaelic proverb:

*"Se obair latha toiseachadh."*

Slowly, Calum reached for a fresh card. On it he inscribed:

FATHER

The battalion sat on a hill behind the lines. On the horizon, they could see the flashes and hear the mutter of the guns. They were going up the lines again at midnight.

It was a calm summer evening. The replacements' knees were pink and their kilts were fresh coloured, stiff and new. They all sat on the hill and waited. They watched the door of the estaminet below. At last it opened.

The CO and the padre came up the hill towards them and stood at last above them. The padre took a piece of paper from the pocket of his neat tunic and licked his lips. The Sergeant Major took a deep breath and bawled:

"Those who wish may fall out!"

Fin got up and walked away from them all to the bottom of the hill.

Down below, Fin turned to greet those who had followed him away from the padre's platitudes.

Nobody else had moved. They all sat, hundreds of them, with their backs turned towards Fin, watching the moving mouth of the elegant padre.

Next day, just after dawn, Fin jumped into the German trench. He landed up to his ankles in the entrails of a living German soldier.

"The point is, I survived."

They shot a boy from the next village, it was not mentioned, he closed his eyes on duty, he went to sleep standing up.

He was listed as "killed by misadventure" in the Honour Roll.

Killed by his own friends; some had blank ammunition in their rifles; did anyone aim over his head?

The bard made a poem about him. . .

On Monday morning he shaved himself using the new foam for which he had paid the equivalent of ten old shillings. The perfume—for which, he now realised, he had bought it in the first place—disappointed him. It smelled like hot metal.

He left the pile of blank cards and went out, without preparing his usual breakfast of muesli and milk. He did not know what he was going to do with the cards now.

Perhaps he should buy some notebooks?

After eating two fried eggs on toast and drinking two cups of coffee in the Italian cafe, he walked along Notting Hill Gate towards the park.

Passing the Russian Embassy he noted a couple in fur coats and hats, talking to the policeman on duty. The policeman was laughing, but the girl looked strained. She ran into the road as though looking for a taxi and then returned to the courtyard.

Inside the park he walked towards Kensington Pond. The water was covered with a thin sheet of ice and a man was feeding the birds from two plastic bags stuffed with bread and toast.

He watched as a tern tried to solve the problem of getting at a slice of bread that had slipped under a sheet of ice. The bird kept pecking at the ghost of the bread and fought off others of its species. Finally, a black-backed gull smashed the ice without realising it was there and sailed off into the park with the food, its wingtips brushing the wet earth.

A dark-haired woman with a fine-boned face and wearing a fur coat strode past athletically, although she was swollen with pregnancy. The mixture of puritanism and sensuality in her features reminded him of his dream.

Years before, when he had first dreamed of the slender strong dark one, he had tried to attach the vision to a real person. She had reminded him of someone he had seen as a child and later, of a girl he had met some years ago in London. But he knew now that she was neither.

Perhaps she was a projection of what Jung called the *Anima*?

He was not sure if he had grasped the theory correctly, but could it not be that the dream woman was a reflection of the feminine side of his nature?

Or perhaps the dream was a precognition of someone whom he was destined to meet? Part of him pooh-poohed this suggestion but another part intuitively felt it was a possibility.

"There are more things between heaven and earth. . ." he would say to himself.

Could this sub-conscious mind attract such a person to him?

*Stupid bastard!*

Later, he picked up one of the stiff cards and wrote on it in block capitals:

ANIMA

A sepia photograph shows the two young people, the laughing man and the full woman in his arms, sitting outside the wooden frame house, the girl wearing the loose dress that does not conceal the curve of her lap.

The woman gazes into the sun and the man bares his teeth at the camera with confidence and love.

"This was taken on the afternoon before the birth."

Later, the boy was to concentrate on his mother's round belly in the picture, taken thousands of miles away in Canada.

He tried to penetrate the veils of tulle and flesh, into the warm darkness where he lay inside her.

Was there some modern machine that could reveal the secret of the photograph to him?

He was in it, yet he was not visible, he was hidden inside the belly of the shingled girl in the picture, buried in the body of a young woman in a trance in a brown photograph.

He shuffled the cards and found the one he had marked:

GRANDMOTHER

He stared at it for a time and then put it down.

Restless again, he went out to roam the street for a time. The public house opposite the park was emptying. The gay pub; and now a shoal of strange and effeminate looking men descended upon him. A man in black lurched near to him, his eyelid flickering once very fast. Some kind of signal?

He went back to the room and began to make two piles of his books and clothes—those he could take easily on the train and those he would leave behind for the housekeeper to get rid of.

He would return to Lewis for the last time. There was nothing now for him in London.

The woman downstairs read him his future in the Tarot before he left:

"The cards are good."

"What about the Devil on the right there?"

"You are holding yourself back. It is in your own hands what you make of the future."

John Calvin would not agree with you, Madam.

He said goodbye to Taff in the pub and promised to write to him. No more stories of the Swansea pubs, Dylan's yellow gloves on the bar, the dehydration of the steelworkers causing their beer to soak through them and form pools on the wooden seats.

The pub in Notting Hill was not real anyway.

He treated himself to dinner on the train. It was more expensive than he remembered and less well cooked.

In the sleeper he recalled the same journey with Helen and her cries as the train gathered speed outside Doncaster. His travelling companion this time was a soldier going home on leave.

The weight began to descend upon him again. . .

He looked out of the plane window as the croft and the sands near his home slipped rapidly past. The land looked dead and wet; the little houses did not belong to it.

He climbed heavily into the taxi for the short journey to the other side of the bay.

*Anything new?*

*Nothing fresh.*

Nothing fresh. . .

# 13

# TOD

He laid the stained fibre suitcase down on the brown grass and surveyed the manure heap. It looked dead and uninviting, was composed of peat ash, dung and blackened straw.

How many times during the past year had Martha walked to the midden carrying peat ash from the fires and scrapings from the floor of the henhouse? Twice a day not including Sundays, of course. Twelve months at fifty equals 600 times. And she had been doing it for many years ever since her return from Canada.

The manure heap had shifted in that time; moved nearer the house and grown smaller, as first the mare, then the cattle, and then the sheep had gone. Now, there were only the rusty hens that scratched about the derelict barn; and the byre full of fishing gear; handlines coiled in round baskets; half-finished lobster pots; aluminium bait trays from the freezer factory in town. There were no fish left in Broad Bay, but cousin Angus refused to face the fact. The crew had found a patch of rough bottom far out which the trawlers feared to tackle; here they occasionally set back the clock of history and hauled on board a stream of fine haddock that tasted as fish used to taste in the dawn of time. It kept them going back.

The stuff in the midden wasn't much good as fertiliser but it would spread on a field soon in any case; the spring carting of the manure was one of the annual rituals that had not quite died out. And had he not, in bright cold December, brought a tractor load of seaweed from the shore to the croft? One load only?

"It will do the vegetables."

Was it only because he liked secretly to observe the old rituals, particularly those of spring? Before bringing out the suitcase of papers, letters and manuscripts, the contents that represented for him the detritus of his entire adult life to date; before fetching the heavy bag, he had dug three plants in around the house; a rhododendron, a cutting of honeysuckle and a forked phallic root picked off a counter in Woolworths: *Will produce a veritable blaze of tiny white flowers in July.*

It was the twenty-second of March. He would have preferred to carry out the task he had planned for so long, on the twenty-first, the actual date of the Spring Equinox. But Saturday was more convenient. And tomorrow was Sunday. His father had died on a Sunday morning, early, at six am, on the day of the Spring Equinox. The twenty-first of March.

He had been lying in bed, awake, busy with a crude sexual fantasy, when his mother burst into his room crying that something was wrong with her husband, his father.

Fin was already dead when he reached his side, lying quietly on his back; the furrows in his face already smoothing themselves out. He had pressed down on the chest, but not very hard; if only he had known the correct technique of heart massage! Much later Beatrice had showed it to him.

"Isn't his skin white!" said the old bosun from the next croft, as he dropped the limp hand back on the bed. He had seen many dead men, no doubt of it.

He went to the henhouse, fetched the graip and began to cut a sheltered place for the fire in the lee of the midden. He had not known the technique for heart massage but he knew exactly how to use the graip, with a double-handed chopping motion, to cut through the matted compost. Who had taught him this?

He decided to burn the manuscript of the novel first of all. The letters could wait. He screwed up some pages, placed them at the back of the fireplace he had cut out of the midden, and struck a match. The paper was thick and slightly damp and refused to ignite. Words and whole sentences caught his attention and he had to force himself not to squat in the cold wind and begin reading. Old images floated into his mind from the book: Shona in her cosy bedroom, waiting for the knock on the window. Did the young people go in for bundling nowadays? What was this use of the foreign word bundling? *Cairis na h'oidhche,* the night watch—and you had to watch out for the old man.

And Monica...Hina...

The novel he was burning revealed the flaw in him as did his use of the subtly incorrect incomer word for *cairis na h'oidhche.* Apart from the terrible defect of being composed of far too much fiction and far too little fact, the book had been written out of a mind that was deeply tainted by Southron values. He had been brainwashed by the cocky English-educated Gaels into denying the truth of his home and culture; and in attempting to give the rest of Scotland and England and the world the picture he and they thought they wanted to see, he had betrayed his heritage. Burn, you time-serving sell-out bastards. He stabbed at the fire viciously with the graip.

The book's theme had some merit, however. Did it not record the beginning of the struggle for individuality and personal truth of someone like himself? Naïve and obvious to a painful degree it certainly was; unforgivably romantic also; but it had been worth the doing at a personal level:

"It will be worth £1,000 of psychiatric treatment to me anyway."

He had said that to a woman in London, before coming home to write in what now appeared as some far off adolescent incarnation.

And much of the book did try to grapple with the tensions peculiar to the island; these tensions that resulted in such high figures for alcoholism and depression (even the diseases of the place are those that are hidden from view...). But island living had a vast credit side too, which no incomer could ever come to grips with: life itself was still seen as a black and white struggle by the people and this gave to all their doings a dignity and a meaning; a depth of thought to their minds. The struggle was no longer with the environment; but then the environment had always taken second place to those things that exist on the hidden side of life.

He fed the growing fire; first with single pages; then with several; last of all with whole chapters. The single pages burned quite well; first they would char at the edges, then brown like ancient manuscripts, finally they burst into flames and ash all at once. He watched the words and sentences and paragraphs and scenes and chapters that had occupied him for years go up in smoke. Cliché.

He stood back and waited for the release to come to him.

Nothing happened. Nothing.

The fire went out, smoored by a lump of grey damp pages. Must be Chapter Nineteen; it had been rather long. . .

He stirred up the heap of manuscript and struck more matches. A page caught fire, rose up and was wafted away, still burning. It landed among some rushes nearby and he impaled it on the graip. More pages were blown away and he pursued them with the fork, like a demented park keeper. All must be consumed. He fried them over the fire with the beginnings of satisfaction; the tines of the graip smoked and were cleansed.

It took some little time to burn the thick pile of pages; typed for him ten years ago by a girl in London who had a glamorous job on a newspaper in Fleet Street; at least, he had thought it glamorous then. Ten pounds was all she had asked for; ten quid for typing a whole novel. She had done it in the firm's time, on the firm's typewriter and thick paper; the thought gave him no satisfaction at all, now. There was a card from Julie among the hundreds of letters in the suitcase; a card announcing the birth of her daughter and asking: "How goes the great novel now?"

Up in flames, my girl, how goes marriage and daughters now?

My work was always more important to me than having any emotional relationship, said the writer, interviewed on BBC2 last night. *A bad case of sex in the head, I would say.*

The letters were neatly tied in bundles and he could tell at a glance which period they represented; in chronological order, backwards, Helen, the Margery interlude, Beatrice. . . Earlier, more innocent friendships provided a mixed heap and then there was the tight faded bundle of the letters to him in New Zealand twenty years ago, from Anne. Had he no letters at all then, from men? There were a few somewhere from a couple of actor friends.

Should he open up the letters, take them out of their distinctive envelopes, spread them individually on the fire? No, much better not; he knew they would affect him more than the re-reading of the dead manuscript.

The writing on the envelopes was so different, so indicative of the personalities of the writers; the tall, sloping script of Helen, with the individual formation of certain letters; the thick sensual strokes of Beatrice; Margery's neat lines that wanted to be larger; the abrupt, impulsive scribble of Anne.

Beatrice had kept a file of his letters to her. At their last meeting, she had handed it to him; he kept it and later re-read the letters. How much good writing energy had he expended on them? These he had already burned, pursued by a Calvanist imp who kept assuring him of his lack of humility; imagine anyone storing his own letters!

What would people think if they found them and him dead under a bus?

Would he ever be free from the terrible sense of shame that haunted the people of Lewis? Why was he burning all this material now? It was not out of shame, whatever the reason.

New beginning, was that it? Did it symbolise the cleaning out of the stable of his unconscious, the preparation of fresh ground where new roots could strike deeper?

All must be consumed...

Did he want to feel free of the past in order to adjust more easily to the new time that was coming to the island? Work on the erection of the repair yard for the oil rigs was far advanced. The jibs of thin cranes poked beyond the skyline across the harbour in the town, dipping and nodding; prehistoric birds in a ritual dance.

*Seventeen feet of peat has to be removed in places.*

The work on the crofts in the villages had not changed much; there was simply very little of it done at all. Few cattle were kept and the land had been invaded by rushes; rushes which throve in a sheep economy.

"I'm just planting a few potatoes this year."

All that was left of the way of life of his grandparents; a hard life but a life of much dignity. *A few potatoes.* His mother had said last week:

"We never had jam, only at rhubarb time."

Yet the crofters clung more tenaciously than ever to their neglected acres; incomers looking for sites for houses in the villages were treated with suspicion and public opinion made it very hard for them to obtain even a quarter acre. And this on an island of a million acres; it was mostly "wet desert" according to the experts, but it must look like paradise to the refugees from the mainland. Were the island people right to be suspicious? Had anything good ever come to them from the South?

Why had he kept so many old programmes? *New Zealand versus South Africa;* green and black jerseys wrestling in the Christchurch mud; the elation in the hotel bar when it became known that a South African prop had suffered a broken jaw...

Rugby is a communal game, as opposed to the fine individualism of football. Was that why he had preferred rugby? Lost in the pack, hidden from view of the spectators. Not that he had been very good at either and when the drink got its grip he stopped playing; or they stopped asking him, he could not be sure which.

Did it matter? He had long ago made his gesture towards the world of the super male and he had failed to stay the course.

The theatre programmes were from much later, from his London period. Strangely enough, the images from the stage were not as vivid as the memory of the moment when he gave Rangi, the elegant Maori loose forward, the pass for the winning try in a long forgotten game. Rangi had since died in an accident on board...

The rituals you take part in are those that really matter. So terrible great care should be taken by all who would preserve and develop their inner integrity.

*So you burn a mound of scrap paper on a dung heap?*

*Aye, it's the symbolism, you see.*

*What symbolism?*

*If I knew, would I not tell you?*

If you knew, you would not have to do it and neither would it be symbolic.

If he had half his life to come, could he not do many things in that time? Plays, novels, poetry, communication? He would take a woman to himself, a permanent partner, a symbol of his desire to communicate and co-operate with people. Should—could?—a person; warm, living, softly receptive, be a symbol? He thought she could...

She was inside himself, in his own mind and all he needed to do was to let go and to permit the transfer of his inner picture of her to the person he was to meet and get to know. He could already visualise her; small, dark, rounded, compact and strong, looking up at him with a challenge and a certainty. . .

A word on a shivering page from a letter caught his eye; he stooped and snatched the leaf from the fire; as he did so, the flames slapped at his face and he felt his hair and eyebrows sizzle. He read Helen's words to him written after she had come, unsummoned, to his rescue in Edinburgh: *I feel so stirred, right to the depths. It will pass, but nothing will blot out the experience of its happening. I think of The Man often. It is like a sequence from a dream.*

He though of The Man now, as he had come to them through the sunshine of dawn in Princes Street gardens; only he and Helen there, on a bench. The ragged figure rose from somewhere and moved painfully towards them along the path. The man was young, but also old, consumed by the cheap wine, the daily communion that had already damaged the peripheries of his body, enclosing him in the agonised extra skin of the chronic alcoholic. His eyes were blue and clear and strange out of the inflamed tissue around them. He stopped in front of this lone couple and stared; their terrible closeness, of the moment only, had resounded upon his supersensitivity.

"One day," he said shakily, "I'll be happy too. With a girl."

He had a soft Gaelic accent.

He fumbled inside the foul and shapeless overcoat and brought out a rosary. Silently, he held it up in front of Tod and Helen.

*Touch it, Helen. . .*

She had done so.

She had done so, though fearful of the emotion suddenly generated between the lost man who was still drinking and the one beside her whom she had helped to save from his relapse: the emotion Tod now let loose upon her.

Weeping on her shoulder and her not ready for it. . .

Is anyone—ever?

He struck a special light.